David Miner
" the consummate
muff diver ! "

GOING DOWN

Lip Service From Great Writers

GOING DOWN

CHRONICLE BOOKS
SAN FRANCISCO

LIBRARY OF CONGRESS CATALOGING-IN-
PUBLICATION DATA:
GOING DOWN: LIP SERVICE FROM GREAT
WRITERS
        P.   CM.
    ISBN 0-8118-2245-1
    1. EROTIC LITERATURE, AMERICAN.
    2. ORAL INTERCOURSE—LITERARY
    COLLECTIONS. 3. EROTIC LITERATURE,
    ENGLISH. I. CHRONICLE BOOKS
    (FIRM)
PS509.E7G65 1998
810.8'03538—DC21   98-35218
                               CIP

PRINTED IN THE UNITED STATES
OF AMERICA.

DESIGNED BY *Sparky Goodman, #58*

DISTRIBUTED IN CANADA BY
RAINCOAST BOOKS
8680 CAMBIE STREET
VANCOUVER, BRITISH COLUMBIA V6P 6M9

10 9 8 7 6 5 4 3 2 1

CHRONICLE BOOKS
85 SECOND STREET
SAN FRANCISCO, CALIFORNIA 94105

WWW.CHRONICLEBOOKS.COM

"When I make love to women I think of their genitals as a, as a ruby fruit jungle."

"Ruby fruit jungle?"

"Yeah, women are thick and rich and full of hidden treasures and besides that, they taste good."
    —RITA MAE BROWN, *Rubyfruit Jungle*

Soon I felt her mouth. I had still a sort of semi hard on. She got it into her mouth and she began to caress it with her tongue. I saw stars.
    —HENRY MILLER, *Tropic of Capricorn*

Introduction

Finally there is a book that collects the best written words on a great oral tradition.

Approaches to oral sex have no doubt been influenced by the words used to describe it. Cunnilingus has to be one of the least appealing and most clinical words in the English or Latin languages, and is impossible to use as a verb; it is nowhere near as evocative as the more vivid muff diving. Fellatio rings more inviting and suggestive, but it sounds like a village in Italy and lacks the immediacy or airiness of, say, blow job. And *soixante-neuf,* or 69, the most melodious of all, is indeed found frequently in these pages, despite its potential for awkwardness. For this volume, we've grouped all these activities under Going Down, a phrase that is geographically explicit yet wonderfully playful.

But where does going down fit in the sexual totem pole? Is it a sign of great devotion and affection, an act of selfless pleasure-giving? Is it true that "to eat another is sacred," as John Updike writes in *Couples*? Or is oral gratification so inconsequential and meaningless that it doesn't count at all: "It is not really adultery if we did not go all the way," says a character in Jill Robinson's *Perdido.*

Going down may not literally be going all the way but it is certainly more than enough for many of the satisfied characters in this anthology. Women and men find equal pleasure under a woman's skirts in excerpts from Erica Jong and Charles Simmons, while an unusual threesome works out quite well in Susan St. Aubin's short story, "Cynthia." And intercourse-free, same-sex get-togethers do not restrict the delights of the men and women in pieces from Oscar Wilde and Cerridwen Fallingstar.

Sometimes oral sex is a prelude to other sexual acts, as told by Norman Mailer and Frank Harris, or for completely different kinds of activity altogether, as described by Frank Zappa. Harold Brodkey shows us it can be a refuge for those who have lost faith in fucking. And discovering others doing it can stimulate the variety of intense emotions recounted by Anaïs Nin, Ken Chowder, and Philip Roth.

In hilarious essays, Anka Radakovich provides tips on technique in "Lip Service: On Being a Cunning Linguist"; and Dan Anderson and Maggie Berman offer "Sex Tips for Straight Women from a Gay Man." Gay Talese, in an excerpt from the nonfiction *Thy Neighbor's Wife*, points out the dependability of the tongue. Rounding out this extraordinary anthology are a quartet of bawdy limericks, the saucy poem "Purple Banana" by Jeremy Reed, and a prose poem in the form of an imaginary letter by Laura Chester.

It's all here: the explicit, the whimsical, the instructional, and—always—the gratifying. For armchair sexual travelers, it doesn't get any better than this.

Anaïs Nin

The Woman on the Dunes

L OUIS could not sleep. He turned over in his bed to lie on his stomach and, burying his face in the pillow, moved against the hot sheets as if he were lying over a woman. But when the friction increased the fever in his body, he stopped himself.

He got out of bed and looked at his watch. It was two o'clock. What could he do to appease his fever? He left his studio. The moon was shining and he could see the roads clearly. The place, a beach town in Normandy, was full of little cottages, which people could rent for a night or a week. Louis wandered aimlessly.

Then he saw that one of the cottages was lighted. It was set into the woods, isolated. It intrigued him that anyone should be up so late. He approached it soundlessly, his footsteps lost in the sand. The Venetian blinds were down but not tightly closed, so he could see right into the room. And his eyes met with the most amazing sight: a very wide bed, profusely covered with pillows and rumpled blankets, as if it already had been the scene of a great battle; a man, seemingly cornered in a pile of pillows as if pushed there after a series of attacks, reclining like a pasha in a harem, very calm and contented, naked, his legs folded out; and a woman, also naked, whom Louis could see only from the back, contorting herself before this pasha, undulating and deriving such pleasure from whatever she was doing with her head between his legs that her ass would shake tremulously, her legs tightening as if she were about to leap.

Now and then the man placed his hand over her head as if to restrain her frenzy. He tried to move away. Then she leaped with great agility and placed herself over him, kneeling over his face. He no longer moved. His face was directly under her sex, which, her stomach curved outwards, she held before him.

As he was pinned under her, she was the one to move within reach of his mouth, which had not touched her yet. Louis saw the man's sex rise and lengthen, and he tried with an embrace to bring her down upon him. But she remained a short distance, looking, enjoying the spectacle of her own beautiful stomach and hair and sex so near his mouth.

Then slowly, slowly she moved towards him and, with her head bowed, watched the melting of his mouth between her legs.

For a long while they maintained this position. Louis was in such a turmoil that he left the window. Had he remained longer he would have had to throw himself on the ground and somehow satisfy his burning desire, and this he did not want to do.

He began to feel that in every cottage something was taking place that he would like to be sharing. He walked faster, haunted by the image of the man and the woman, the round firm belly of the woman as she arched herself over the man . . .

Then he reached the sand dunes and complete solitude. The dunes shone like snowy hills in the clear night. Behind them lay the ocean, whose rhythmic movement he could hear. He walked in the white moonlight. And then he caught sight of a figure walking before him, walking fast and lightly. It was a woman. She wore some kind of cape, which the wind billowed like a sail, and seemed propelled by it. He would never catch up with her.

She was walking towards the ocean. He followed her. They walked in the snowlike dunes for a long while. At the ocean's edge, she flung off her clothes and stood naked in the summer night. She ran into the surf. And Louis, in imitation, discarded his clothes and ran into the water also. Only then did she see him. At first she was still. But when she saw his young body clearly in the moonlight, his fine head, his smile, she was not frightened. He swam towards her. They smiled at each other. His smile, even at night, was dazzling;

hers, too. They could scarcely distinguish anything but the brilliant smiles and outlines of their perfect bodies.

He came closer to her. She let him. Suddenly he swam deftly and gracefully over her body, touching it, and passing on.

She continued to swim, and he repeated his passage over her. Then she stood up, and he dove down and passed between her legs. They laughed. They both moved with ease in the water.

He was deeply excited. He swam with his sex hard. Then they approached each other with a crouching motion, as if for a battle. He brought her body against his, and she felt the tautness of his penis.

He placed it between her legs. She touched it. His hands searched her, caressed everywhere. Then again she moved away, and he had to swim to catch her. Again his penis lay lightly between her legs, then he pressed her more firmly against him and sought to penetrate her. She broke loose and ran out of the water, into the sand dunes. Dripping, shining, laughing, he ran after her. The warmth of the running set him on fire again. She fell on the sand, and he over her.

Then at the moment when he most desired her, his power suddenly failed him. She lay waiting for him, smiling and moist, and his desire wilted. Louis was baffled. He had been in a state of desire for days. He wanted to take this woman and he couldn't. He was deeply humiliated.

Strangely enough, her voice grew tender. "There is plenty of time," she said. "Don't move away. It's lovely."

Her warmth passed into him. His desire did not return, but it was sweet to feel her. Their bodies lay together, his belly against hers, his sexual hair brushing against hers, her breasts pointed against his chest, her mouth glued to his.

Then slowly he slipped off to look at her—her long, slender, polished legs, her rich pubic hair, her lovely pale glowing skin, her full breasts very high, her long hair, her wide smiling mouth.

He was sitting like a Buddha. She leaned over and took his small wilted penis in her mouth. She licked it softly, tenderly, lingering over the tip of it. It stirred.

He looked down at the sight of her wide red mouth so beautifully curved around his penis. With one hand she touched his balls, with the other she moved the head of the penis, enclosing it and pulling it gently.

Then, sitting against him, she took it and directed it between her legs. She rubbed the penis gently against her clitoris, over and over again. Louis watched the hand, thinking how beautiful it looked, holding the penis as if it were a flower. It stirred but did not harden sufficiently to enter her.

He could see at the opening of her sex the moisture of her desire appearing, glistening in the moonlight. She continued to rub.

The two bodies, equally beautiful, were bent over this rubbing motion, the small penis feeling the touch of her skin, her warm flesh, enjoying the friction.

She said, "Give me your tongue," and leaned over. Without interrupting the rubbing of his penis, she took his tongue into her mouth and touched the tip of it with her own tongue. Each time the penis touched her clitoris, her tongue touched the tip of his tongue. And Louis felt the warmth running between his tongue and his penis, running back and forth.

In a husky voice she said, "Stick your tongue out, out."

He obeyed her. She again cried, "Out, out, out, out . . ." obsessively, and when he did so he felt such a stirring through his body, as if it were his penis extending towards her, to reach into her.

She kept her mouth open, two slender fingers around his penis, her legs parted, expectantly.

Louis felt a turmoil, the blood running through his body and down to his penis. It hardened.

The woman waited. She did not take in his penis at once. She let him, now and then, touch his tongue against hers. She let him pant like a dog in heat, open his being, stretch towards her. He looked at the red mouth of her sex, open and waiting, and suddenly the violence of his desire shook him, completed the hardening of his penis. He threw himself over her, his tongue inside of her mouth, and his penis pressing inside of her.

But again he could not come. They rolled together for a long while. Finally they got up and walked, carrying their clothes. Louis' sex was stretched and taut, and she delighted in the sight. Now and then they fell on the sand, and he took her, and churned her, and left her, moist and hot. And as they again walked, she in front of him, he encircled her in his arms, and threw her on the ground so that they were like dogs coupling, on their hands and knees. He shook inside of her, pushed and vibrated, and kissed her, and held her breasts in his hands.

"Do you want it? Do you want it?" he asked.

"Yes, give it to me, but make it last, do not come; I like it like this, over and over and over again."

She was so moist and feverish. She would walk, waiting for the moment he would thrust her into the sand and take her again, stirring her and then leaving her before she had come. Each time, she felt anew his hands over her body, the warm sand against her skin, his caressing mouth, the caressing wind.

As they walked, she took his erect penis into her hand. Once she stopped him, knelt before him and held it in her mouth. He stood towering over her, with his belly moving slightly forwards. Another time she pressed his penis between her breasts, making a cushion for it, holding it and letting it glide between this soft embrace. Dizzy, palpitating, vibrating from these caresses, they walked drunkenly.

Then they saw a house and stopped. He begged her to conceal herself among the bushes. He wanted to come; he would not let her leave until then. She was so aroused and yet she wanted to hold back and wait for him.

This time when he was inside of her he began shaking, and finally he came, with a violence. She half climbed over his body to reach her own fulfillment. They cried together.

Lying back resting, smoking, with the dawn coming upon them, lighting their faces, they now felt too cool and covered their bodies with clothes. The woman, looking away from Louis, told him a story.

She had been in Paris when they had hanged a Russian radical who had killed a diplomat. She was then living in Montparnasse, frequenting the cafés, and she had followed the trial with a passion, as all her friends had done, because the man was a fanatic, had given Dostoevskian answers to the questions put to him, faced the trial with great religious courage.

At that time they still executed people for grave offenses. It usually took place at dawn, when no one was about, in a little square near the prison of the Santé, where the guillotine had stood at the time of the Revolution. And one could not get very near, because of the police guard. Few people attended these hangings. But in the case of the Russian, because emotions had been so much aroused, all the students and artists of Montparnasse, the young agitators and revolutionaries had decided to attend. They waited up all night, getting drunk.

She had waited with them, had drunk with them, and was in a great state of excitement and fear. It was the first time she was to see someone die. It was the first time she was to see someone hanged. It was the first time she was to witness a scene that had been repeated many, many times during the Revolution.

Towards dawn, the crowd moved to the square, as near as the rope, stretched by the policemen, would allow and gathered in a circle. She was carried by the waves of crowding and pushing people to a spot about ten meters away from the scaffold.

There she stood, pressed against the rope, watching with fascination and terror. Then a stirring in the crowd pushed her from her position. Still, she could see by standing on her toes. People were crushing her from all sides. The prisoner was brought in with his eyes blindfolded. The hangman stood by, waiting. Two policemen held the man and slowly led him up the stairs of the scaffold.

At this moment she became aware of someone pressing against her far more eagerly than necessary. In the trembling, excited condition she was in, the pressure was not disagreeable. Her body was in a fever. Anyway, she could scarcely move, so pinned was she to the spot by the curious crowd.

She wore a white blouse and a skirt that buttoned all the way down the side as was the fashion then—a short skirt and a blouse through which one could see her rosy underwear and guess at the shape of her breasts.

Two hands encircled her waist, and she distinctly felt a man's body, his desire hard against her ass. She held her breath. Her eyes were fixed on the man who was about to be hanged, which made her body painfully nervous, and at the same time the hands reached for her breasts and pressed upon them.

She felt dizzy with conflicting sensations. She did not move or turn her head. A hand now sought an opening in the skirt and discovered the buttons. Each button undone by the hand made her gasp with both fear and relief. The hand waited to see if she protested before proceeding to another button. She did not move.

Then with a dexterity and swiftness she had not expected, the two hands twisted her skirt round so that the opening was now at the back. In the heaving crowd, now all she could feel was a penis slowly being slipped into the opening of her skirt.

Her eyes remained fixed on the man who was mounting the scaffold, and with each beat of her heart the penis gained headway. It had traversed the skirt and parted the slit in her panties. How warm and firm and hard it was against her flesh. The condemned man stood on the scaffold now and the noose was put around his neck. The pain of watching him was so great that it made this touch of flesh a relief, a human, warm, consoling thing. It seemed to her then that this penis quivering between her buttocks was something wonderful to hold on to, life, life to hold while death was passing . . .

Without saying a word, the Russian bowed his head in the noose. Her body trembled. The penis advanced between the soft folds of her buttocks, pushed its way inexorably into her flesh.

She was palpitating with fear, and it was like the palpitation of desire. As the condemned man was flung into space and death, the penis gave a great leap inside her, gushing out its warm life.

The crowd crushed the man against her. She almost ceased breathing, and as her fear became pleasure, wild pleasure at feeling life while a man was dying, she fainted.

After this story Louis dozed off to sleep. When he awakened, saturated with sensual dreams, vibrating from some imaginary embrace, he saw that the woman had gone. He could follow her footprints along the sand for quite a distance, but they disappeared in the wooded section that led to the cottages, and so he lost her.

Philip Roth

Portnoy's Complaint

S MOLKA comes back into the kitchen and tells us she doesn't want to do it.

"But you said we were going to get laid!" cried Mandel. "You said we were going to get blowed! Reamed, steamed, and dry-cleaned, that's what you *said!*"

"Fuck it," I say, "if she doesn't want to do it, who needs her, let's go—"

"But I've been pounding off over this for a week! I ain't going anywhere! What kind of shit is this, Smolka? Won't she even beat my *meat?*"

Me, with my refrain: "Ah, look, if she doesn't want to do it, let's go—"

Mandel: "Who the fuck is she that she won't even give a guy a hand-job? A measly hand-job. Is that the world to ask of her? I ain't leaving till she either sucks it or pulls it—one or the other! It's up to her, the fucking whore!"

So Smolka goes back in for a second conference, and returns nearly half an hour later with the news that the girl has changed her mind: she will jerk off one guy, but only with his pants on, and that's *all*. We flip a coin—and I win the right to get the syph! Mandel claims the coin grazed the ceiling, and is ready to murder me—he is still screaming foul play when I enter the living room to reap my reward.

She sits in her slip on the sofa at the other end of the linoleum floor, weighing a hundred and seventy pounds and growing a mustache. Anthony Peruta, that's my name for when she asks. But she doesn't. "Look," says Bubbles, "let's get it straight—you're the only one I'm doing it to. You, and that's it."

"It's entirely up to you," I say politely.

"All right, take it out of your pants, *but don't take them down.* You hear me, because I told him, I'm not doing anything to anybody's balls."

"Fine, fine. Whatever you say."

"And don't try to touch me either."

"Look, if you want me to, I'll go."

"Just take it out."

"Sure, if that's what you want, here . . . here," I say, but prematurely. "I-just-have-to-get-it——" Where *is* that thing? In the classroom I sometimes set myself consciously to thinking about DEATH and HOSPITALS and HORRIBLE AUTOMOBILE ACCIDENTS in the hope that such grave thoughts will cause my "boner" to recede before the bell rings and I have to stand. It seems that I can't go up to the blackboard in school, or try to get off a bus, without its jumping up and saying, "Hi! Look at me!" to everyone in sight—and now it is nowhere to be found.

"Here!" I finally cry.

"Is that it?"

"Well," I answer, turning colors, "it gets bigger when it gets harder . . ."

"Well, I ain't got all night, you know."

Nicely: "Oh, I don't think it'll be all *night*—"

"Laydown!"

Bubbles, not wholly content, lowers herself into a straight chair, while I stretch out beside her on the sofa—and suddenly she has hold of it, and it's as though my poor cock has got caught in some kind of machine. Vigorously, to put it mildly, the ordeal begins. But it is like trying to jerk off a jellyfish.

"What's a matter?" she finally says. "Can't you come?"

"Usually, yes, I can."

"Then stop holding it back on me."

"I'm not. I am trying, Bubbles—"

"Cause I'm going to count to fifty, and if you don't do it by then, that ain't my fault."

Fifty? I'll be lucky if it is still attached to my body by fifty. *Take it easy,* I want to scream. *Not so rough around the edges, please!*— "eleven, twelve, thirteen"—and I think to myself, *Thank God, soon it'll be over—hang on, only another forty seconds to go*—but simultaneous with the relief comes, of course, the disappointment, and it is keen: this only happens to be what I have been dreaming about night and day since I am thirteen. At long last, not a cored apple, not an empty milk bottle greased with vaseline, but a girl in a slip, with two tits and a cunt—and a mustache, but who am I to be picky? This is what I have been imagining for myself . . .

Which is how it occurs to me what to do. I will forget that the fist tearing away at me belongs to Bubbles—I'll pretend it's my own! So, fixedly I stare at the dark ceiling, and instead of making believe that I am getting laid, as I ordinarily do while jerking off, I make believe that I am jerking off.

And it begins instantly to take effect. Unfortunately, however, I get just about where I want to be when Bubbles' workday comes to an end.

"Okay, that's it," she says, "fifty," *and stops!*

• • •

"No!" I cry. "More!"

"Look, I already ironed two hours, you know, before you guys even got here—"

"JUST ONE MORE! I BEG OF YOU! TWO MORE! PLEASE!"

"N-O!"

Whereupon, unable (as always!) to stand the frustration—the deprivation and disappointment—I reach down, I grab it, and POW!

Only right in the eye. With a single whiplike stroke of the master's own hand, the lather comes rising out of me. I ask you, who jerks me off as well as I do it myself? Only, reclining as I am, the jet leaves my joint on the horizontal, rides back the length of my torso, and lands with a thick wet burning splash right in my own eye.

"Son of a bitch kike!" Bubbles screams. "You got gissum all over the couch! And the walls! And the lamp!"

"I got it in my eye! And don't you say kike to me, you!"

"You *are* a kike, Kike! You got it all over everything you mocky son of a bitch! Look at the doilies!"

It's just as my parents have warned me—comes the first disagreement, no matter how small, and the only thing a *shikse* knows to call you is a dirty Jew. What an awful discovery—my parents who are always wrong . . . are right! And my eye—it's as though it's been dropped in fire—and now I remember why. On

Devil's Island, Smolka has told us, the guards used to have fun with the prisoners by rubbing sperm in their eyes and *making them blind*. I'm going blind! A *shikse* has touched my dick with her bare hand, and now I'll be blind forever! Doctor, my psyche, it's about as difficult to understand as a gradeschool primer! Who needs dreams, I ask you? Who needs Freud? Rose Franzblau of the *New York Post* has enough on the ball to come up with an analysis of somebody like me!

"Sheeny!" she is screaming. "Hebe! You can't even come off unless you pull your own pudding, cheap bastard fairy Jew!"

Hey, enough is enough, where is her sympathy? "But my eye!" and rush for the kitchen, where Smolka and Mandel are rolling around the walls in ecstasy. "—right in the"— erupts Mandel, and folds in half onto the floor, beating at the linoleum with his fists— "right in the fucking—"

"Water, you shits, I'm going blind! I'm on fire!" and flying full-speed over Mandel's body, stick my head beneath the faucet. Above the sink Jesus still ascends in his pink nightie. That useless son of a bitch! I thought he was supposed to make the Christians compassionate and kind. I thought other people's suffering is what he told them to feel *sorry* for. What bullshit! If I go blind, it's his fault! Yes, somehow he strikes me as the ultimate cause for all this pain and confusion. And oh God, as the cold water runs down my face, how am I going to explain my blindness to my parents! My mother virtually spends half her life up my ass as it is, checking on the manufacture of my stool—how am I possibly going to hide the fact that I no longer have my sight? "Tap, tap, tap, it's just me, Mother—this nice big dog brought me home, with my cane." "A *dog*? In my house? Get him out of here before he makes everything filthy! Jack, there's a dog in the house and I just washed the kitchen floor!" "But, Momma, he's here to stay, he has to stay—he's a seeing-eye dog. I'm blind." "Oh my God! Jack!" she calls into the bathroom. "Jack, Alex is home with a dog—he's gone blind!" "Him, blind?" my father replies. "How could he be blind, he doesn't even know what it means to turn off a light." "How?" screams my mother. *"How? Tell us how such a thing—"*

Mother, how? How else? Consorting with Christian girls.

Mandel the next day tells me that within half an hour after my frenetic departure, Bubbles was down on her fucking dago knees sucking his cock.

The top of my head comes off: "She *was?*"

"Right on her fucking dago knees," says Mandel. "Schmuck, what'd you go home for?"

"She called me a kike!" I answered self-righteously. "I thought I was going blind. Look, she's anti-Semitic, Ba-ba-lu."

"Yeah, what do I give a shit?" says Mandel. Actually I don't think he knows what anti-Semitic means. "All I know is I got laid, *twice.*"

"You *did?* With a *rubber?*"

"Fuck, I didn't use nothing."

"But she'll get pregnant!" I cry, and in anguish, as though it's me who will be held accountable.

"What do I care?" replies Mandel.

Why do *I* worry then! Why do I alone spend hours testing Trojans in my basement? Why do I alone live in mortal terror of the syph? Why do I run home with my little bloodshot eye, imagining myself blinded forever, when half an hour later Bubbles will be down eating cock on her knees! Home——to my mommy! To my Tollhouse cookie and my glass of milk, home to my nice clean bed! *Oy,* civilization and its discontents! Ba-ba-lu, speak to me, talk to me, tell me what it was like when she did it! I have to know, and with details——exact details! What about her tits? What about her nipples? What about her thighs? What does she do with her thighs, Ba-ba-lu, does she wrap them around your ass like in the hot books, or does she squeeze them tight around your cock till you want to scream, like in my dreams? And what about her hair down there? Tell me everything there is to tell about pubic hairs and the way they smell, I don't care if I heard it all before. And did she really kneel, are you shitting me? Did she actually kneel on her *knees?*

And what about her teeth, where do they go? And does she suck on it, or does she blow on it, or somehow is it that she does *both?* Oh God, Ba-ba-lu, did you shoot in her mouth? Oh my God! And did she swallow it right down, or spit it out, or get mad—tell me! what did she do with your hot come! Did you warn her you were going to shoot, or did you just come off and let *her* worry? And who put it in—did she put it in or did you put it in, and does it just get *drawn* in by itself? And where were all your clothes?—on the couch? on the floor? exactly *where?* I want details! Details! Actual details! Who took off her brassiere, who took off her panties—her *panties*—did *you?* did *she?* When she was down there blowing, Ba-ba-lu, did she have anything on at all? And how about the pillow under her ass, did you stick a pillow under her ass like it says to do in my parents' marriage manual? What happened when you came inside her? Did she come too? Mandel, clarify something that I have to know— *do* they come? Stuff? Or do they just moan a lot—or *what?* How does she come! What is it like! Before I go out of my head, I have to know what it's like!

Anka Radakovich

Lip Service: On Being a Cunning Linguist

MOST men love oral sex. They love receiving it, that is. Giving it is another story. My experience, and that of my girlfriends, has led me to the conclusion that only half of the male population are cunnilingual enthusiasts. This statistical data is confirmed by the two-to-one ratio of men on the streets of New York who scream "Blow me!" as opposed to "Sit on my face!"

The reasons for such ambivalence toward this activity are numerous. Some men are so anxious to stick it in that they bypass cunnilingus altogether. Others are selfish and don't get much satisfaction from giving someone else pleasure. Our culture traditionally teaches men to conquer and women to serve, so a man may be uncomfortable taking a submissive stance. Consequently, when a man is on his knees it's easier to see if he's selfish or if he has any real interest in our pleasure. It also lets us see what he would look like with a mustache.

Another often-cited excuse for lack of enthusiasm is the occasional aroma. This is perfectly understandable. I myself have put my head between a pair of legs, intending to drive someone wild with my oral skills, only to stop myself after catching one whiff of a scent closely resembling a urinal. I therefore can sympathize with someone who does not want to lick something that may at times seem like a wedge of limburger cheese with a bad toupee.

On the other hand, I salute the other 50 percent of the male population, true oral fans. I'll never forget the first time someone dove between my legs. Unfortunately, it didn't happen until I was twenty-three years old. I was breaking in the front seat of my new car and got so excited by the tingling sensation that I accidentally hit the gearshift and plowed right into the garage door, smashing the front end. (Imagine explaining this one to the insurance adjuster.)

One orally ambidextrous boyfriend specialized in pearl diving. In fact, that's all he wanted to do. This was fine with me. I appreciated his jubilant attitude and made sure to cheer him on with shouts, or "Nobody licks my monkey like you do!" After a month of this, I became tongue-whipped (the female equivalent of pussy-whipped), and even offered to do his laundry if he would come over and satisfy me. After two months, I put a framed photo of his tongue on my desk.

One reason the sport of muff diving is not practiced more often than women would like it to be is that some men don't know how to do it. To some men, female anatomy is still a mystery. For them, I offer a few tips. First, take the gum, cigarette, or toothpick out of your mouth. If you wear glasses, take them off so they won't get fogged up. If you are worried about feminine hygiene, spread some Tic Tacs down there.

Start by kissing and talking to her like Barry White. Then head for the breasts. Suck those. For some women, the nipples are directly connected to the genitals. Once you've discovered the fertile crescent, locate the clitoris so you can see what you're doing. (It's the tiny pink thing on top that doesn't kiss back but really likes you.) Since every woman is different, it helps to have an inventory of techniques. Practice does help, but training on a peach would make anyone feel like a loser. Try the "silken swirl" or the "Baskin Robbins." Whatever you do, keep your tongue moving. This will only lead to voluntary reciprocation. In addition to oral moves, some women occasionally like a finger or two inserted into the love nest. A frisky nose is always welcome, as is a "Miami Vice"–stubbled chin. Refrain from inserting teeth, fists, or feet.

Avoid putting direct pressure on the little man in the canoe until it seems very aroused. Signs of escalating excitement include moaning, grunting, and threatening to commit suicide if you stop. Then head right to the love button. Signs that she's having an orgasm range from heavy breathing to fingernails digging into your back to convulsions. If you see her eyes rolling back in her head or hear shouts of "Hallelujah!" you can be sure you did something right.

One note: Since women are multiply orgasmic, oral sex is just the beginning of the encounter, a sort of tantalizing appetizer to the zucchini entrée. Many prefer having an orgasm by something more probing, and let's face it, not too many have eight-inch tongues.

Where to perform cunnilingus is another story. Hanging from a chandelier is a logical location. Another good place is the kitchen sink. This can have its disadvantages, however, like the time I tried it and ended up repeatedly banging my head against the toaster.

The 69 position is more awkward for women. Working out the logistics of fitting mouths of orifices and protrusions while adjusting to the rhythm is like playing a game of Naked Twister. This position further emphasizes the intimate-yet-impersonal contradictory nature of oral sex. With 69, a side-by-side position is recommended over a top-and-bottom position to avoid accidental death by asphyxiation, a lesson to be learned from the 400-pound woman I read about in the *Weekly World News* who suffocated her husband to death when she sat on his face.

Once the thrill of cunnilingus is gone, the after-kiss slowly approaches. It's not that the scent of our own womanhood bothers us, but smelling ourselves is a reality check. At this moment, a handshake is better than a kiss.

Susan St. Aubin

Cynthia

ANNE climbed the back steps to Richard's apartment one Friday evening and peered through the window in the kitchen door before knocking. This time Richard wasn't waiting for her alone, running his left hand through his short gray curls as he read papers from his literature classes, he was drinking coffee with a tall, slender woman dressed in a gray skirt and white silk blouse tight over her small round breasts, her dark hair tied off her face with a piece of black velvet ribbon. She was perhaps in her mid-forties, but it was hard to tell: when she threw her head back and laughed, she was like a girl of sixteen, and when she looked down at her veined hand on the table and frowned, she was like a woman of fifty. She got up and went to the sink with her coffee cup, moving like a dancer, her clinging flannel skirt showed the ripple of her muscles.

Anne remembered then that she'd seen her in front of Richard's apartment building the first time she'd gone there six months ago. The woman had been waiting for a cab, which pulled up as Anne rang Richard's doorbell; she'd thought nothing of it at the time, though the woman had stared at her with penetrating black eyes as if she knew Anne, just twenty years old, wearing jeans and a tight blue tee-shirt, was on her way to her first affair with a professor.

It began to rain lightly. Richard looked up to check the clock on the wall above the door, saw her, and jumped to his feet. "Anne, come in! You're early." He opened the door with one hand while the other played with his hair. The woman turned around and leaned against the sink, smiling.

"Not so very early," said Anne. "It's almost five."

"Anne, this is Cynthia."

Cynthia held out her hand. "I was just leaving. How nice to meet you at last. I've heard so much about you."

Anne was startled by the coldness of her fingers; her smile, too, seemed cold. Richard went with Cynthia to the front door. When he came back, Anne was sitting at the kitchen table staring at her brown boots. He lifted her long blond hair off her neck and pulled it gently over one shoulder, stroking it like the pelt of an animal. "Why don't you take off your coat? Cynthia's a very old friend. I wish you wouldn't come creeping up the back stairs like that, you might see all sorts of things you'd rather not."

Anne stood up to take off her coat. Richard ran his hand over her breasts, then kissed her, sliding his tongue between her lips and teeth, which she opened somewhat reluctantly, still brooding about Cynthia. She knew she wasn't the only student he invited to his flat; their Friday nights were just one night out of seven, and they occasionally exchanged smiles when they passed in the school corridors. She allowed him to lead her to the bedroom.

"You're still upset, aren't you?" He unbuttoned her dress, let it slide to the floor, pulled her slip over her head, pulled her tights down over her hips, and knelt before her to kiss her mons. She held her legs together, but felt herself loosen as his tongue worked its way between the folds.

He undressed, and they lay on the waterbed in the middle of the room while he stroked her breasts with one hand and her cunt with the other, fingers dipping into her wetness, until she came with a shudder, one hand stroking and clutching his penis. Then he slid his penis inside her and she gripped it with her vaginal muscles, gripping and relaxing rhythmically until he came; and the force of his coming so excited her that she came again, unexpectedly, gasping, then laughing.

"Why did you laugh?" He seemed disturbed.

"When I get something I don't quite expect, I sometimes do." She looked up at the Indian print cloth with tiny mirrors woven into the fabric which he had tacked to the ceiling above the bed like a canopy, while he slowly stroked her breasts and belly. After a while they got under the covers and slept.

In the night she felt him kissing and rubbing against her; she felt his penis grow hard against her buttocks as he stroked her breasts from behind. She reached back and guided him into her cunt. He kissed her lips and stroked her face and breasts. But how could that kiss be his if he were behind her? There were two hands on her breasts, different hands, one slimmer and smoother than the other; the hands stroked and clasped one another as much as they stroked her. She felt smooth straight hair brush across her face and breasts. Then she came with more intensity than she had ever known, and was unconscious.

Later she woke briefly and felt herself between two bodies. She assumed that she was still dreaming, that the other incident had been a dream, and that this was a continuation of that dream. She slipped into dreamlessness.

In the morning she woke alone in Richard's big bed with sunlight pouring in the window: they'd forgotten to close the curtains. She could hear his coffee grinder whirring in the kitchen, water running, and the clatter of cups. When she shut her eyes, she noticed a scent that was neither hers not Richard's, a sweet musk that seemed to permeate the sheets. She remembered her dream, that sense of another body, a woman's body, in bed with them.

Richard brought her a cup of coffee, and carefully sat on the edge of the bed with his mug.

"I had a dream," she said.

"Oh?" He seemed to have anticipated this conversation.

"I dreamed there was a third person in bed with us, a woman, I think, but I'm not sure. I was making love with you, and then there was this other person kissing me, and you, and stroking both of us."

He smiled. "Sounds like something you'd like to do, maybe. Dreams are just fantasies of all the things we don't allow ourselves to do in real life."

"No, I don't think so—it's something I've never thought of." She watched the steam rise from her coffee cup.

"The dream means you must have, at some level. Dreams don't lie."

She was still troubled. "The funny thing is, it didn't feel like a dream."

He snorted. "What do you mean, feel like?"

"My dreams usually feel like dreams. I always know when I've been dreaming. But this—I know it must have been a dream, it couldn't have happened, but it didn't feel like a dream. It was real."

He laughed. "Come on, it was a dream. I've had dreams like that before, everyone has. The dream you think must have been real is probably the dream you most want to be real."

"I've never had a dream like this."

"Then it's your first. I've been present for lots of your firsts, haven't I?" He put her coffee cup gently on the floor beside his before getting into bed with her. "I'll have to find us another woman just to keep you happy."

"You're putting dreams in my head, that's what it is! *You* want another woman with us." Though she laughed into his armpit, she half believed what she was saying.

"Is it something you might want to try?"

She shook her head. "No."

"Think about it."

She shook her head again.

But she did think about it after she left his house at noon; she thought about it for the rest of the week. Before her biology class she asked Nina, who was five years older and claimed to be bisexual, if she'd ever made love with a man and a woman together. Nina dropped her pen and bent under the desk to get it. Sitting up red and flushed, she said, "No, I never wanted to; sex is too personal a thing for me. I've been asked, but no orgies." She spoke very fast; other students were coming into the lecture hall.

Later, Nina asked her if this was something Richard wanted to do. Nina was the one person Anne had told about Richard, and she seemed to disapprove of the relationship, though Anne couldn't think why. Now she said to Anne, "Don't let yourself be pushed into something you can't handle. Be sure you know what you want, that's all. Don't let Richard talk you into it."

Anne nodded. "I won't. But it's something I've been thinking of, too; it's not just an idea he put in my head." She thought of her dream, the dream she almost suspected Richard of planting in her mind, if such a thing were possible. But even if he had, he had created a desire within her which she now felt was her own. "He did suggest it," she admitted to Nina, "but only because I had a dream about it."

Nina lifted her eyebrows. "Oh? Well, in that case . . ." She laughed. "I definitely think you should pay attention to dreams."

"Or pay attention to what you want to do," said Anne. "Even if someone else suggested it first."

It was windy on the lawn where they sat. Anne's hair blew up behind her head like a huge yellow fan, and Nina's short bronze curls twisted and turned. Anne was thinking of Cynthia; she was certain Cynthia was the woman she had dreamed about.

• • •

"There is one woman I'd like to make love to, with you," she told Richard that Friday. "Cynthia."

He ran his left hand through his hair and smiled. "I'd like to invite you to dinner together. I'm sure she'd enjoy talking to you. But you can't push anything. If we feel like going to bed together, that's fine, and if not . . ." He trailed off. They made a date for two weeks from Saturday.

"Is Saturday her night?" Anne asked.

Richard laughed. "I'm not quite that obsessive."

Anne dreamed of Cynthia for the next two weeks. On the Saturday of their dinner date, Anne bathed and dressed with extra care, putting on a long beige dress of a nylon fabric that clung to her breasts and body. Over the dress she wore a mohair scarf of a lighter beige and a long trench coat. She looked at her reflection in the mirror on the door to her room as she left, and added a mohair hat that matched the scarf.

When she got to Richard's, Cynthia was already there, very elegant in a brown and beige striped skirt and bronze blouse, her straight brown hair falling loose on her shoulders. She was slicing tomatoes for a salad at the kitchen counter. Richard wore his jeans, as he always did on the weekends. Anne sniffed the familiar aroma of Richard's specialty, chicken stuffed with cashews and French bread crumbs. Cynthia greeted her with a smile, as though she already knew Anne quite well, though Anne had only met her once, and took Anne's hand in both of hers.

"I've brought some strawberries," she said. "Do you want to help clean them?"

Anne was glad to have the strawberries to wash. She carefully cut the stem from each one, then sliced them and covered them with brandy and a little sugar.

"A dessert salad," she said to Cynthia.

Richard had set the table, and sat in the middle with Anne and Cynthia at either end.

"Wonderful chicken," said Cynthia. "I'd forgotten how wonderful."

Richard smiled at her. "More stuffing?" he asked Anne.

"The stuffing's Richard's invention," Cynthia explained to Anne. "I love French bread, so we always had leftover stale ends of it in the house."

There was an uncomfortable silence as Anne realized they must have lived together. For a moment, she felt like an intruder in their home.

"Now I just buy a loaf and use it fresh," said Richard.

Cynthia laughed. "Yes, and it tastes so much better this way." She got up, cleared their plates, and brought the bowl of strawberries to the table. "Would you like to dish them up?" she asked Anne, and Richard put three small cut-glass dishes beside the bowl.

Anne spooned the strawberries and syrup into a bowl for Cynthia, then Richard, before serving herself. After they finished eating, Richard lit a cigarette while Cynthia cleared the table and poured them each a cup of coffee, which they sipped in silence. When Anne looked anxiously at Richard, he smiled at her. Cynthia looked from one to the other and laughed.

"Why are we being so silly?" she asked. She put her hand on Anne's. "Richard has told me everything about you, but I see he's told you nothing of me, which may be just as well."

Richard looked out the window.

Anne looked at Richard, then Cynthia.

"Have you ever made love to a woman?" asked Cynthia.

"No," Anne answered.

"Never?" Cynthia smiled and raised her eyebrows.

They sat silently around the table a bit longer. Richard still looking out the window, Cynthia looking at Anne, and Anne looking down at her hands folded around her coffee cup, listening to her own breathing, which seemed the loudest sound in the room. Richard got up and went into the bedroom; after a bit, Anne and Cynthia followed. While Richard lay nude on the bed, watching and smoking a cigarette, Anne and Cynthia undressed in a quick, business-like fashion, like going to the doctor, Anne thought. She watched Cynthia take off her skirt, her silk blouse, her half slip.

Richard stood up to stroke Cynthia's shoulders, then unhooked her brassiere from behind. Anne thought she had a very nice body, smooth skinned, slender, still lightly tanned from the summer. She saw one small white breast released from its lace cup, and then, where the other should be, a white scar across her chest. Anne felt her breath stop, then catch, then start. Of course mastectomies were common; her own mother had had one, yet she had never seen the scar. It wasn't nearly as bad as she had imagined: some horrible disfiguration, the breast chopped away, leaving a gaping hole or a circle of red scar tissue like a burn. Cynthia's neat white scar, leaving no trace of breast, barely noticeable beneath her brassiere, was something Anne hadn't been prepared for. She gently touched the breast, caressing the nipple, which hardened under her palm.

"You see," said Cynthia, "I still have one."

Anne's fingers traced the scar.

"Yes, I had cancer, of course. The usual reason. They told me I had no choice. I think they were right; as it was I . . ." Here she stopped as though there were something she could not admit just yet. To Anne she looked very healthy, but perhaps she was not expected to live.

Anne kissed the scar. "Does it hurt?"

"No, not now."

Anne fastened her mouth to the nipple and circled it with her tongue, sucking lightly and thinking of her mother, who had never revealed her scar. Cynthia stroked Anne's hair. It seemed to Anne that Richard had disappeared; she wanted no one but Cynthia. Then she felt him behind her, his swollen penis poking the small of her back as he reached around to her breasts.

The three of them moved to the bed, where Anne lay back while Richard and Cynthia stroked her breasts. It was like being an infant, she thought, cared for by a mother and father, but what parents these were! While Richard massaged and licked her breasts, Cynthia ran her tongue down Anne's belly, moving it rapidly in and out of her navel, continuing down to her mons, blowing gently in the light brown pubic hair while sliding her tongue around the clitoris.

Anne heard herself moan. Never had she felt such a certain knowledge of her body and its response from a lover. As Cynthia flicked her tongue over the tip of Anne's clitoris, they both began to breathe faster. Richard sat by Anne's head stroking her hair and her breasts while she moaned and twisted and then called out, feeling as though she had been struck by a flash of lightning that went all the way through her and out her toes.

She panted and swallowed; her throat was very dry. Cynthia lay on top of her, her breast soft and the other half of her flat and hard as a man. Anne stroked her shoulders. They rolled over and lay on their sides, still stroking, until slowly Anne slid one hand between Cynthia's legs.

She had never touched another woman like this before. It was so much like touching herself, but with no sensation, that she was frightened. She felt as if she were numb; she could feel nothing but a moist softness on her fingers, like the inside of a sun-ripened peach or plum. It must be like this, she thought, to know braille, to read a book with your fingers. She had to learn through her fingers what pleased Cynthia. Tracing over the hood of the clitoris, she heard Cynthia moan. The right side moved her more than the left; a finger sliding around the opening to the vagina was as pleasurable for her as it was for Anne. Slowly she tested the area, remembering what she liked; and what she liked, Cynthia seemed to like. The soft sensation of ripe fruit was becoming a part of her: when she touched Cynthia, she could feel herself grow swollen and wet, and moved her fingers, still wet from Cynthia's cunt, to her own while she bent her mouth to Cynthia's clit and, as Cynthia had to hers, flicked it with her tongue.

The taste was the same taste of a man, only more intense, more salty and fish-like, with a sweetness quite unlike the bitterness of sperm. Hesitant at first, Anne stuck her tongue deeper into the folds, and finally thrust it into the vagina, testing, tasting. Richard lay on the other side of Cynthia, and while Anne was tasting the new soft fruit, she stroked Richard's hard penis. She moved her lips back to Cynthia's clit again, while with one hand she guided Richard's penis from behind into Cynthia's cunt. Anne kept her thumb and forefinger circled firmly around the base of his thrusting penis while she continued to stroke Cynthia's clit with her tongue.

Cynthia moaned, then screamed: Anne followed her as she thrashed about, never stopping even when she came, but going on while she climaxed again and again, stronger each time, until she was very still, gasping for breath. Richard withdrew then, and Anne took his penis in her mouth while Cynthia's fingers stroked her clit. Richard's penis still tasted of Cynthia; when he came she sucked and swallowed his sperm, which seemed to have a little of Cynthia's sweetness mixed with his bitterness. They fell asleep all three together, Anne in the middle. When Anne woke at dawn, Cynthia was gone, as though she'd been a dream. She snuggled closer to Richard and slept again.

In the morning she asked Richard why Cynthia had left.

"I don't think she'll be back," he told her. "I think she's done what she wanted to." He refused to say more, so she didn't push him.

On her own she looked for Cynthia—on campus, in stores, on

the street. She realized she knew nothing about her; she didn't know where she worked, what she did, or where she lived. Once in a downtown department store she thought she saw her standing erect in a rust-colored, clinging dress, talking to the woman behind the jewelry counter, but when she turned around, it wasn't Cynthia.

Without Cynthia, Anne found her relationship with Richard uninteresting. Gradually they saw less of one another; she heard he had a new young girlfriend and didn't care, except when she thought the two of them might make love with Cynthia. Richard was her link to Cynthia; she realized she would most likely never meet Cynthia again except through him. She asked him about her the last Friday they were together.

"I haven't heard from her," he said sharply, but with sadness. "I think she's gone away."

"Where?"

"I don't know." He shrugged. "She didn't say."

"Away from the city?"

"Oh, yes. She's not here anymore."

"But didn't she tell you where?"

"No." He got up to carry their cups to the sink. Anne knew their relationship had nothing more for her, and mourned the loss of Cynthia more than the loss of Richard.

• • •

She grew friendlier with Nina. When spring semester started, they had lunch together on the lawn almost every day. Anne never spoke of Richard, but one day Nina asked if she still saw him.

"No," said Anne. She looked up at two seagulls circling in the clear sky just above them. "I think I'm in love with a woman friend of his."

Nina lay on the grass, her chin cupped in the palms of her hands. "Oh, yeah?"

"But I haven't seen her in months." Anne wasn't sure if she should tell Nina about the night she'd spent with Richard and Cynthia, but decided to go ahead. At the first mention of Cynthia, Nina sat straight up.

"He knows another woman named Cynthia?" she asked.

"I only know this one, I didn't know there was another." And Anne went on with her story, putting in details of their lovemaking she thought would be particularly exciting to Nina. She even told of Cynthia's scar, and of her feeling of fear at first, then acceptance, even an erotic acceptance, of Cynthia's deformity.

"But that's extraordinary," said Nina. "That can't be! You see, I knew Richard's wife. Her name was Cynthia. She died about seven years ago, of breast cancer."

Anne felt her heart jump. "He never told me he'd been married, he never said anything about a wife."

"But the woman you described, that's Cynthia, his wife. If it weren't impossible, I'd say it was her. How amazing, he's actually gone and found somebody just like her." Nina pulled blades of grass from the lawn and piled them beside her knee. "He probably called her Cynthia because she looked like his wife. Maybe he even made her have a breast amputated so she'd be Cynthia all over again. No, that's ridiculous. The whole thing is ridiculous." She continued to pick at the grass, looking down at her hand. "You see, Cynthia, his wife, was my first lover. I was fifteen. She was my ballet teacher. She'd been a dancer with the San Francisco Ballet, a very minor dancer, but to me she was wonderful; I'd never met anyone like her before. And Richard was—well, in the way. I never liked him, I could never understand why she didn't just leave him. But she loved him." Nina looked at Anne. "They were in love. There's not many couples you can say that about, and have it mean anything. And then, after I'd known her a few months, she had her surgery and my parents sent me away to school in Vermont—they figured out what was going on and couldn't get me off the West Coast fast enough. Three years later when I came back, she was dead. And Richard was playing around with students, but not me. He really wanted me, of course, in memory of Cynthia I guess. But no way, I could never stand him."

While Nina talked, Anne remembered the texture of Cynthia's skin, the feel of her hair as it brushed across her arm. It was as if Cynthia were there with them on the lawn. Anne felt her hands tighten into fists. "Do you believe in ghosts?" she asked Nina. "Do you think such a thing is possible, I mean Cynthia coming back to make love with us?"

"No, I don't. Though it's just the kind of thing she would do." Nina smiled. "No, I don't believe it, but I do believe Richard is looking for his wife, and found a woman just like her, and called her Cynthia. That's what I believe."

Anne lay on her back and looked at the sky. The seagulls were gone. When she shut her eyes she felt something like silk brush her leg, and smelled Cynthia's perfume. She opened her eyes. Nina was a few feet away, staring into the grass, her eyebrows pressed together.

Anne felt the ghost of Cynthia rise from her mind and disappear like a mist. Real or not, she was gone now. Nina's hair was golden red in the sun. Anne could almost feel the heat of its color. She rolled closer.

Limericks

There was a young fellow named Meek
Who invented a lingual technique.
   It drove women frantic
   And made them romantic,
And wore all the hair off his cheek.

A canny Scotch lass named McFargle,
Without coaxing and such argy-bargle,
   Would suck a man's pud
   Just as hard as she could,
And saved up the sperm for a gargle.

There was a young bounder named Link
Who possessed a very tart dink.
    To sweeten it some
    He steeped it in rum,
And he's driven the ladies to drink.

Old Louis Quatorze was hot stuff.
He tired of that game, blindman's buff,
    Up-ended his mistress,
    Kissed hers while she kissed his,
And thus taught the world *soixante-neuf.*

Norman Mailer

Harlot's Ghost

I DISPATCHED the letter before second thoughts could com-
mence. Then I went back to my hotel room and tried to sleep,
but the sheets reeked of Sally, formaldehyde, and me. She
always left behind a strong odor of herself, half carnal and half
grudged out of existence by her deodorants, which didn't always
take care of the job.

I hardly knew what to do about Sally. We were more intimate
than our affection for each other. And my derelictions of duty were
increasing. If Porringer was working triple-time under Hunt, I took
time out from my own double-time to arrange a meeting with Chevi
Fuertes which I knew would not take place. I had not notified him.
Instead, I saw Sally. A week later, I did as much again.
Professionally speaking, it was easy to conceal. Agents often
missed meetings. Like horses, they bolted at the sight of a leaf

blowing by. I had to file bogus reports, but they were routine, and bought two hours each time with Sally in my bedroom at the Cervantes. I, waiting for her, would have my clothes off, and my bathrobe on; she, knocking on the door with a tap followed by two taps, would be out of her shoes and off with her skirt even as we embraced in the first of her powerful kisses. "Glue sandwiches" I would have labeled them if not in the mood, but I was usually in the mood, and, naked in a streak, we grappled toward the bed, stealing handfuls of each other's flesh en route before diving down into the song of the bedsprings, her mouth engorging my cock. There are a hundred words, I suppose, for a penis, but cock is the one that goes with fellatio, and her open marriage with lust, abandonment, and sheer all-out hunger for Hubbard's Yankee prong gave that fellow a mind of his own, a hound off his leash, a brute pillaging the temple of her mouth, except who could call it a temple?—she had confessed to me in one of our postcopulatory conversations that from high school on, she had had a natural appetite, or was it thirst, for this outpost of the forbidden, and, God, it was out of control by the time she came to me.

I, in turn, was developing tastes and inclinations I did not know I had. Before long, she was presenting her navel and pubic hair toward me, and I, facing the contradictory choices of domination or equality, found my own head reaching to explore her sandy, almost weedlike bush. I am cruel enough to mention how wild and scraggly it looked because that came to mean little. It was the avid mouth behind the hair that leaped out to a part of me that did not know it existed until I was licking and tonguing away with my own abandon which I had never known could belong to my critical lips until they opened into the sheer need I knew to jump across the gap from one bare-ass universe to the next. The only way I ever felt close to Sally Porringer was when her mouth was on my cock and my face was plastered into the canyon between her legs. Who could know what things we had to tell each other at such times? It was not love we exchanged, I expect, but all the old bruises and pinched-off desires—how much there was of that! Lust, I was deciding, had to be all the vast excitement of releasing the tons of mediocrity in one-self. (Then, afterward, when alone in my bed, I would wonder if new mediocrity had been ingested just as much as the old had been purged.) I was discovering that I had the gusto of a high school athlete and the chill estimates of a man so noble in perception of each unhappy nuance as T. S. Eliot.

Say this for the act. When we rose dripping from the sweet and sour mire of feeding on each other, my copulation came pounding happily out of me. To fuck fast was to throw one's heart into the breach and pound enough blood to the head to banish Thomas Stearns of the Eliot family. One gunned the motors of one's soul and the sugar of one's scrotum—what a joy to discover that Hubbards also secreted scrotum sugar—up, up, over the hill, and into the unchartable empyrean beyond. That vision seemed to disappear almost as soon as it afforded its glimpse. I would be happy for a while to know I was a man and that she wanted me and I gave her pleasure. Soon enough she would be stirring once more. She was not insatiable, but near enough. By the third time, I would be thinking again of Lenny Bruce, and the worst of all this passion was not its successive blunting, but the knowledge that when we were done, we would not know how to talk. We were about as essentially happy with each other in this situation as two strangers who attempt to make conversation on a train.

Whatever the shortcomings, two days later, I would want her again. It was hardly an environment in which to write to Kittredge, but some jobs have to be done.

Jill Robinson

Perdido

H E is waiting for me in front in a shirt open to the waist and jeans. He gets in the car.

"Where do you want to go?"

"Let's just go. Anywhere," he says. He puts his hand on my thigh. "When you have fantasies what do you think about?"

"Being a sort of girl Woody Guthrie with fringed sequins. . . ." I know that's not what he means but I want to hear it from him.

"That's not what I mean and you know it. Don't play Susie Sunshine with me."

"Okay, don't play James Dean. What do you want to do?"

"I want to watch you drive. Go out to Mandeville, then up where you were that night."

"Of the fire? I'm not going there."

"Why not?" He's put his hand on my breast and is rubbing it lightly with his palm.

"Because. Because there's a subdivision. And it's also too far. I don't want to tease any more. Let's just do it and never talk about it, can you do that?"

"Can you?" He leans behind me at a light and lifts up my hair, brushing his lips at the back of my neck.

"Yes." I could do anything. He does not just look and talk. He knows. It's going to happen to me today with a man and that is all I am thinking about.

"Go up Franklin Drive," he says, "up above the Beverly Hills reservoir. I'm going to lie you down and look at your big, blond body until you're so hot you can't even tell me where to start on you." He is talking in his lowest, wildest voice, projecting across the front seat now from where he's looking at me over in the corner, arm out the other window, projecting so well that it sounds as if he is talking inside my own body, sounds like the dream orders I give myself. It feels like a dream. This cannot be something I would do. That is how to see it.

And we are up in the soft hills above Beverly. He leans over and turns off the motor just as I've stopped and I smell the sweet, heavy scent of his hair and he lifts his face up to mine and grabs my hair pulling my head down and his mouth is softer, wetter than I thought it would be and with our mouths still closed he darts his tongue side to side fast across my lips, and doing it firmer and firmer yet he puts his hands on my breasts and draws them up until his fingers are turning my nipples right through my bra and I feel all the feelings I've felt by myself, but more.

I grasp the tops of his thighs with my hands, rubbing along down the long muscles hard with my thumbs, moving closer and closer. This is like the sex you get from certain musical hooks where it builds and builds and breaks and builds again above the breaking point. Our eyes half closed and staring at each other, we swallow and grasp hands and let go, moving—looking at each other—out of the car, and he walks around to my side and grabs my hand again and runs with me to a flat grassy place where we stand, our arms down at our sides, hands clenched into each other's hands and press our bodies together rubbing and digging into each other in long deep circles and then he slides down to his knees and rubs his face against me, then clasps my knees with his arms and pulls me down. I cannot lie still, my body lifts and lifts to him. He slides off my jeans and we laugh at each other in the dirty husky laugh of teenagers as he sees I have no underpants on. He pulls off the jeans and I unbutton my shirt, flinging it, and it lands on a bush and I throw off my bra and lie back with my arms and legs out wide. I reach up then and toss my hair all out around me in a fan and lie with my arms raised under my head, watching as he takes off his shirt and his jeans and we laugh again to see he also has no shorts on.

"Now," he says, "I'm going to do you. But if you move I'll stop. I want to get you crazy. I'm going to start you and stop you and start you and stop you and when you can't stand it I'll stop you and start again. . . . If you move around I'll stop." And he kneels between my legs and starts at me with his hands. He knows he knows. I knew he had to know. And every time I writhe he takes his hands away and pins down my hips with them and starts again, one breast, then the other, nibbling until I look to see if I have lit all up with the heat and flashlight brightness of the feeling, and all the time he keeps coming back with his hand, stopping me, starting me.

"I've looked at you and thought, someone's got to do her, man, before that chick explodes. . . ."

"Oh, yeah. More, more." I feel like I feel when I watch a great jazz drummer, like when we danced that time and I watched the drummer's jaws move with his gum and the beat. And then when I'm limp and the sweat's coming down in ribbons around my face and pouring into my hair and my back is arching and I'm thrusting down on his hand and lifting my legs, curving them around his shoulders, he puts his jaw down to me and does what he did with my mouth with his tongue and it's like fiddles just shimmering off in my head and everything is going down deeper, harder, down to a dirty chord that will not quit and this is sex, this is it, this is what the shouting and the crying and the wailing and the rhythm and the jazz and all of that's about and he feels the feeling coming down right down there, grouping up and he presses his face, down, with the mouth, such a mouth he's got, and his hands go in for the finish which goes off like the brass section's all standing up and he's done me, done me, and I wrap my legs around his shoulders and bend up from the waist clutching his head with my hands and bending down over him. "Jesus, thank you, oh my God, that's been forever coming like that."

"It just takes having a lot of interest in your work." He's straddling me, his knees at my waist now and his hands on the ground on either side of my head. I reach forward and grasp his lean, tan hips and move him up into my mouth, moving up and around and gliding, circling in and out, with my hands holding tight, and then one hand holding him steady, the other going around between his thighs, feeling the soft, swinging weight of him, stopping him, starting him, teasing him and coming back for more until he's leaping, fuller, fuller, and he's grabbing my hair pulling it around like reins, pulling it tight against my cheeks as I draw him down and out and he howls like that coyote howled up on that other hill when he was thinking about having me and watching me all those years ago.

We lie side by side clutching hands. We do not look at each other.

We do not talk about it. Or why or what it means or whether we should or shouldn't have or if we'll do it again. It started and happened and ended as something separate from either of our realities. Separate from each other almost. Like fantasies colliding in midair the way radio stations sometimes catch into each other and then right themselves into their assigned wavelengths. It had, undoubtedly, to do with the past, but not the present. Or the future.

Here's selective morality; it is not really adultery if we did not go all the way.

Jeremy Reed

Purple Banana

Her finger trick creates a banana:
it is ophidian how he erects
and telescopes into her lipsticked pout
and undulates a slow motion
in and out, not a sixty-nine,
she crouched down on her haunches, bottom up
in air-sheer white panties.

She imagines a tongue teasing her crack
and he additional fingers on his balls,
they need inventives to participate
in sensory extravagance;
the weird conjunction of geometries,
two side by side, one flipped over,
the other on his back.

He eases his purple banana free
before it shoots its seeding galaxy.
Fellatio as an aperitif
stimulates the volcanic impetus
to other pleasures.

   She ascends a scale
of excruciating laughter;
it's guess work what he does to her
and where he is and over and over
their tensions twist around a molten core.

Frank Zappa and
Peter Occhiogrosso

Girls Together Outrageously

THE overall stylistic concept of the GTO's had a lot to do with Christine Frka. Unfortunately, she OD'd sometime during the 1970s—I don't know exactly when.

Christine was the one who recommended that I record Alice Cooper, and later provided them with the ideas for their costumes. (When I first saw them, they looked pretty much like a bunch of guys from Arizona.)

Christine used to hang out with Miss Sparkie, Miss Mercy, Miss Pamela, Miss Lucy, Miss Sandra and Miss Cynderella. They were totally dedicated and devoted to every aspect of rock and roll—especially the part about guys in bands who had Big Weenies.

Miss Mercy's claim to fame at that time was an unusual interest: *butter*. She used to open the refrigerator, remove a quarter-pound stick, and swallow it whole. Miss Sandra always carried a small can of Crisco for personal lubrication.

The only other thing that mattered to them was the concept of *raw, unbridled costumery.* There was strong competition between the ladies as to which one was dressing in the most "unique" way. (If you can still find it, *Permanent Damage,* the album of the GTO's, manages to give a pretty good flavor of their lifestyle.)

Included in it is a tape of Cynthia Plaster-Caster talking on the phone to Miss Pamela (now known as Pamela *"I'm With the Band"* Des Barres), comparing notes. They both kept diaries, so they had cross-references to the same guys. Noel Redding, bassist from the Jimi Hendrix group, also kept diaries, intertwined with the other two. It would have been great to see them all in one book.

It's unfortunate that the only diaries published so far have been Pamela's. Good as they are, they're not nearly so well written or insightful as Cynthia's.

I met Cynthia Plaster-Caster when the Mothers were working as the opening act for Cream at the International Amphitheatre in Chicago in 1968. This was toward the end of Cream's existence, when all the guys in the band hated each other. Each guy had his own road manager, his own limousine, his own etc., etc., etc.

During a conversation backstage, Eric Clapton asked if I had ever heard of the Plaster-Casters. I said I hadn't. He said *"Well after the show, come with me. You won't believe this."* So, we went to his hotel.

Upon arrival we found, sitting in the lobby, two girls. One of them had a small suitcase with an oval cardboard emblem glued to the side that said *"THE PLASTER-CASTERS OF CHICAGO."* The other one had a brown paper bag.

They didn't say a word—just stood up and followed us into the elevator, and into the room. The suitcase girl opened the suitcase. The other opened the bag. They took out some "statuettes": *"Here's Jimi Hendrix, and here's Noel Redding, and here's the roadie from. . . ."*

They put them on the coffee table and took out the rest of their gear—everything a person might need to make a plaster replica of *the human weenus.*

We spent two or three hours talking with them. Neither of us volunteered to be "immortalized."

The Plaster-Casters were written up in various publications at that time. Probably as a result of this, our office received a portfolio from a guy who claimed to be doing something similar with *female organs,* casting them in silver. Very nice.

The material used for the molds in each case was the same stuff the dentist puts in your mouth for taking impressions of your teeth. It's a powder called alginate, which, when mixed with water, gets rubbery, and eventually hardens so that plaster can be poured into it.

The way the Plaster-Casters worked was, one of them would mix the goo while the other one gave the guy a blow job. As you can imagine, this sort of thing requires a scientific sense of timing.

The blow-job girl had to take her mouth off the guy's dick at the precise moment the other one slammed the container full of glop onto the end of it, holding it there until it hardened enough to make a good mold. Cynthia wouldn't blow the guys; that was the other girl's assignment. Cynthia mixed the goo.

Meanwhile, the "subject" had to concentrate on maintaining an erection, otherwise he wouldn't *make a good impression*.

When Hendrix was cast, Cynthia told me, he liked the glop so well, he *fucked the mold*.

Frank Harris

My Life and Loves

As I lay in bed that night about eleven o'clock I heard and saw the handle of the door move: at once I blew out the light; but the blinds were not drawn and the room was alight with moonshine. "May I come in?" she asked. "May you?" I was out of bed in a jiffy and had taken her adorable soft round form in my arms. "You darling sweet," I cried and lifted her into my bed. She had dropped her dressing-gown, had only a nightie on and in one moment my hands were all over her lovely body. The next moment I was with her in bed and on her; but she moved aside and away from me.

"No, let's talk," she said. I began kissing her but acquiesced: "Let's talk." To my amazement she began: "Have you read Zola's latest book *Nana*?" "Yes," I replied. "Well," she said, "you know what the girl did to Nana?" "Yes," I replied with sinking heart.

"Well," she went on, "why not do that to me? I'm desperately afraid of getting a child, you would be too in my place, why not love each other without fear?" A moment's thought told me that all roads lead to Rome and so I assented and soon I slipped down between her legs. "Tell me please how to give you most pleasure," I said and gently, I opened the lips of her sex and put my lips on it and my tongue against her clitoris. There was nothing repulsive in it; it was another and more sensitive mouth. Hardly had I kissed it twice when she slid lower down in the bed with a sigh whispering: "That's it; that's heavenly!"

Thus encouraged I naturally continued: soon her little lump swelled out so that I could take it in my lips and each time I sucked it, her body moved convulsively and soon she opened her legs further and drew them up to let me in, to the uttermost. Now I varied the movement by tonguing the rest of her sex and thrusting my tongue into her as far as possible; her movements quickened and her breathing grew more and more spasmodic and when I went back to the clitoris again and took it in my lips and sucked it while pushing my forefinger back and forth into her sex, her movements became wilder and she began suddenly to cry in French, "oh, c'est fou! oh, c'est fou! oh, oh!" and suddenly she lifted me up, took my head in both her hands and crushed my mouth with hers as if she wanted to hurt me.

The next moment my head was between her legs again and the

game went on. Little by little I felt that my finger rubbing the top of her sex while I tongued her clitoris gave her the most pleasure and after another ten minutes of this delightful practice she cried, "Frank, Frank, stop! kiss me! Stop and kiss me, I can't stand any more. I am rigid with passion and want to bite or pinch you."

Naturally I did as I was told and her body melted itself against mine while our lips met—"You dear," she said, "I love you so, and oh how wonderfully you kiss."

"You've taught me," I said. "I'm your pupil."

Ken Chowder

Jadis

Egg had been a cheerful baby. He sang while he ate and there exists an album littered with portraits of his toothless grin. He came home from kindergarten with a proud announcement: "I'm one of the yucky ones who got to take thpeech." Even then his days always had their amiable if opaque purpose. "Where are you going, Egg?" "Gonna go into the yiving." "What are you going to do there?" "Gonna yook around." All right, Egg: go ahead and yook.

It was impossible to tell whether his temper produced his good luck or luck induced his good temper. At any rate, his luck held and held. His birth itself was a lucky accident; his mother was forty-three at his birth, and described her new baby as her "do-it-yourself grandchild." His home had been full of serenity and lovely music; his parents treated him tenderly; he was natural heir to all the toys in the world. He grew up short but healthy, had abbreviated and perfect cases of mumps and measles, swam beautifully, and learned to read in nursery school. His bones never broke; his flesh never knew a stitch, nor his teeth a filling. He played every down for a football team that lost every game, and losing was his preference.

So it seems obvious that Egg, far from being snakebit, was an impossible target for a cottonmouth to get fangs into. The snake made neat punctures in the toe of Egg's flimsy running shoe, but Egg had retained from childhood the habit of buying clothing and shoes a bit too big for him, as if he were still hopeful of growing. The fangs went into the shoe's toe, but Egg's own toes were farther back. He felt the impact of the strike in his foot, but he didn't stop running, and he didn't even see the snake until he looked back again and saw something wriggling feverishly on the path. Then he did stop; he looked at his shoe, saw the two surgically neat holes in canvas, and took off at top speed.

He reached the ranger station safely. He dropped the daypack, pulled off his cotton shirt, now a wet rag, and lay down on the grass. He lay quietly, waiting for his heart to slow, but the damn thing would not stop beating. Soon his wet back on grass grew itchy; the presence of this trivial bodily reaction comforted him, as if it could signify the resumption of normalcy and reaffirm the old pleasurable fact of existence. He scratched vigorously, but this was a savage, relentless itch. His back had been lashed by a hundred tiny whips. He started off in the direction Tory and Quammie had taken, still feverishly clawing at his flesh.

The path plunged into woods as deep as a jungle. Thick palm trees crowded around steaming pools of luridly chartreuse water. The air was cooler here, but dark and close; in a few places sunlight barreled in, but the light was captured, held, strangled, and finally extinguished in the depths of the forest. From close by Egg heard, or thought he heard, the repetitive whooping of a chimpanzee. A second chimp whooped on the opposite side of the path, and he began to hurry through the dark forest, impelled by anxiety and by another emotion that he was unhappy to name. Uncommon in him, this was horror—a loathing for the mind that had codified the brutal natural laws. Survival of the fittest, the fascism of nature. The organization of the world—wherein lions thoughtlessly ripped the throats out of antelopes, and humans consciously anticipated their deaths all life long—was a fiendish contraption, the work of a masterful and boundlessly cruel genius. But at that moment the path broke free from the jungle, a salty breeze cleared the laden air, and he came upon a long vista of dunes and long grass as familiar, sensible, and calm as Cape Cod. Rattlesnakes enjoyed sunning themselves quietly in these grassy dunes, but Egg did not know this. He heard the plash of distant breakers and saw seagulls smoothly gliding back and forth, while high in the sky a piece of pale moon, flecked with blue, serenely drifted. Like a boy racing ahead of his parents, Egg ran, feet churning sand and arms wind-milling at his sides, up to the brow of the last dune; he looked out over an endless, perfectly flat, bone-white beach—where small waves peacefully furled and fell, then with a hiss pulled tiny shells softly out to sea.

But that was not all Egg saw.

He saw Tory and Quammie.

Immediately he ducked behind his neighborhood dune. Because of what he'd seen he considered staying behind it. But Inch by inch he scuttled like a crab back up the dune; at the top he hid his face in a sheaf of beach grass and looked out at the scene below.

Tory was spectacularly naked. Her coppery body glistened with oil, which brought out warm highlights on the roundnesses of contour abounding on her—this global breast, this mobile shoulder, these matching pelvis bones that stretched taut the skin of the stomach. All of these parts were Tory, and they were all undulating; she was dancing. Smiling, she made gentle waves with both arms, first on one side, then the other, very Hawaiian; then without a slip of her smile she bumped and ground, calling attention with flagrant sliding hands to those parts of her that needed no second introduction; she disco-danced and cancanned, she leapt and twirled. All the while the only music was the fall of waves and the faint hiss after, with a gull's occasional catcall; all the while she smiled at Quammie, while the old man sat in the deep sand at the foot of a dune and happily wiggled his toes. From time to time Quammie raised his binoculars to his eyes, backward, so as to see—Egg, could imagine it without trouble—a miniature Gauguin: a tiny honey-colored Tory dancing in the distance, waves frothing in back of her, moon and sky behind.

He tried thinking of this as an amusing and absurd spectacle, like something out of a Fellini movie: a young woman cancanning on a deserted beach for the amusement of a funny old man and a hundred seagulls. He went so far as to adopt a pleased little smile. He tried to elevate this into a smirk, but the mouth wouldn't curl any farther, and after a while it dropped into a straight line. Tory's smile, in contrast, was wide, bold, and apparently happy. She'd been a topless dancer, and Egg wondered whether this happiness was a trick she'd learned then, like a doctor's bedside manner, or whether she was actually enjoying herself, and enjoying Quammie enjoying her—because this was a form of love. This too was love.

He kept on watching, wishing he weren't. He saw Tory naked and began to remember and wish. He remembered her close beside him in his high-school Valiant car; they parked by the reservoir, dolphin-blue water and her sweet mouth, they spent long hours in that car, deep green dusk and the musky smell of her neck, they merely held each other, close stars bright white and the warmth between her legs.

If it hadn't been Tory on the beach, but someone else; if she hadn't smiled so happily; even if she'd just danced more quietly and less well, and moved less like water under wind—then he could have watched the jiggle of boobs and the bob of buttocks without the baggage of emotion. But it was Tory, and her parody of sexuality was stunningly sexual. She approached Quammie, smiling, her brown round bottom still rolling in time with interior rhythms; still smiling, she knelt in front of the old man and briefly fumbled with his brief shorts; then her head dropped, and her glossy black hair fell and spread over Quammie's heavy and lucky thighs. Egg among the beach grass groaned and closed his eyes against the sight. He had come all this way to discover, for the first time in his life, some very old and unoriginal sins. Jealousy. Envy.

A few minutes later Tory in black bikini hopped happily among the waves. Egg rounded the dune and greeted Quammie. "Ah," Quammie said, with satisfaction. "Our sandwiches have arrived. Did you have a good walk?"

"An alligator came after me."

Quammie smiled at this. "Did he? Good. How did you manage to get away?"

"I ran."

"An alligator could outrun you, my friend. I very much doubt that its heart was in the chase. Did you stamp your foot?"

"Oh, I stamped my foot all right. I don't think the damn alligator would even have noticed me if I hadn't. But when it finally did notice, it headed right over."

"That," Quammie said, "was surely an alligator that people have fed once too often. Humans regard the world as one large zoo."

"A snake tried to kill me too," Egg said. He held up his running shoe. "It just missed my toes."

Quammie examined the two holes. "Splendid," he said. "It didn't happen to inject venom into your shoe, did it? You know, you are twice blessed. You're the first man I've found who could induce an alligator to give chase. Also one of the very few struck by a snake. I know one fellow who, in the interest of science, has been the willing target of reptiles, but you are the first accidental and seemingly innocent victim. My heartiest congratulations."

"It was nothing," Egg said.

Tory came running up the beach, beaming, hands full of bright things. She began speaking long before she could be heard. ". . . endless supplies of whole sand dollars, which must make the local sandman very rich. This is called angel's wing, which is just what it looks like of course, and this is a moon snail, and these are my favorites: lettered olives. There are sea horses here too, sometimes."

"Hippos on campus," Quammie said.

"How was your walk? I'm glad you finally showed. I'm completely starving. Ravenous."

"Ravishing," Quammie added.

"Yes. I'll bet you are," Egg said grimly. It sounded so unlike him that Tory stared. Egg would have stared at himself if this had been physiologically possible, and if he could have disengaged his gaze from the depths of Tory's navel, into which he had once inserted the tip of his tongue. It had just fit.

"Lovely pears," Quammie said. "Had we Gorgonzola cheese, all would be invincibly right with the world."

The next morning Quammie returned to work. He put in a dozen hours daily. He wrote with a sharp pencil, in a tiny hand, on index cards; in moments of happiness with work accomplished he would shuffle his finished cards, making them jump like seals. Then it was Professor Quammie's great pleasure to return the cards to their correct places in the lineup. As he did, he felt like God casually rearranging the universe on a day off.

It was Quammie's opinion that he was not a great scientist,

and perhaps not a scientist at all. He was a popularizer. He was a genius, of course, but there were many geniuses. True scientists positioned themselves on the tip of some tiny branch of the tree of knowledge: at that moment a genuinely great scientist would be splicing genes, or synthesizing hormones from viruses, or colliding positrons and electrons, or distinguishing mutagens from carcinogens, or calculating distances to quasars, or determining the flavors of quarks, or, at the very least, saving the humble snail darter. He was a pop scientist, more a master of ceremonies than a talent. But he loved science; he loved all natural systems; he loved the astounding intricacy of the world and of every outlandish creature in it. He had been married five times, he loved women, but biology was the true love of his life. And from time to time he found that perceived time took a sudden leap; he looked up from his lectern as if awakening in a new world, then looked down and found on an index card a perfect, or adequately perfect, description of, say, the symbiotic relationship between the handsome yucca plant and some dreary bug. At times like these Quammie forgave himself a week of mediocrity and a month of ill temper.

After breakfast that morning Quammie pulled the red linen napkin from his neck, tossed it breezily onto the table, and retired to his study—with the air of a man about to face for the millionth time the reality of experience, or forge in the smithy of his soul the uncreated conscience of the human race, or else spend a solid hour on the toilet reading *People* magazine.

Tory suggested to Egg that they take a tour of the town. "It's very small, it'll only take a minute. We can buy some crabs or fish at the dock."

McClellanville was composed of a hundred wooden houses, mostly white. Huge live-oak trees, draped with veils of Spanish moss, lined the streets. A slanting church, fast asleep. A school, oddly silent. One antiquated grocery store, with a dog napping on the wooden steps, and the screen door creaking as it slowly swung despite the absence of human impetus. This wasn't a sunny day, but it was hot all the same. Thick, morose clouds circled above, closing in.

On impulse Egg yanked a piece of Spanish moss from a passing tree and twirled it around Tory's head. "A makeshift crown," he proclaimed. "A laurel wreath. A garland for poor drowned Ophelia."

"Very nice," she said. "But I think I'll pass. I hear that fleas live in that stuff. Also lice."

"What, no ticks?"

"Also ticks. We're big on ticks here," she said. He laughed. "Not a joke," she said. "Check the backs of your knees before you go to bed."

The McClellanville Shrimp Company's warehouse jutted over the water. Tory and Egg walked into its cavernous, fish-reeking darkness. Their heels on the wooden floor produced sounds that echoed about the place, but no one came out of the darkness to sell fish. Tory opened one of the long, low freezers and stirred in its ice. "Hell, I can never tell one kind of fish from another."

Idly he put his hand too among the chips of ice. He was aware of Tory beside him; with an effort, he put his mind on other things. "Feels good," he said, speaking of the ice. "I feel like jumping in and waiting for winter to come."

"Go ahead, jump in. Frozen Egg. I'll call your mother and let her know her long suffering is over."

"Where is everybody?"

"They're around. They probably know it's me and are hiding in a back locker. Let's take a seat." She pointed to the far end of the warehouse, which opened above the river. They sat on the edge of the dock, dangling their legs. Terns and pelicans were both out in force, diving for fish. The terns swooped and sailed, elegant as swallows. The pelicans began well enough, flying with gangling necks tucked into shoulders, but when it came time to dive, their cover was blown—they would backpaddle with flailing wings as if uncertain whether to go head or feet first, whether to dive at all, and when they finally splashed awkwardly down they just sat on the water, looking like cantankerous old men in a sulk.

"Why should the warehouse men hide if they know it's you?"

Egg asked, as if he'd been considering this the whole time. In fact he'd been thinking about something quite different, and asked this question to avoid the unspoken subject.

Tory's eyebrows gathered. "What do you think? Two Yankees buy a house that's belonged to the same family for about ninety-three generations. One of them is over seventy, the other a nymph, a wood nymph, of thirty-three. They live flagrantly out of wedlock. And then there's my questionable racial background."

"Not questionable. Exotic."

"In Westchester I'm exotic. Here I'm questionable. So," she said, "would you guess we'd be welcomed with the keys to the city?"

"Because it's you, yes," he said, with an extra beat of the heart, but she didn't respond to his gallantry. "So what do they do to you?" he asked.

"They don't *do* anything," she said. "We're not talking about white robes and pointy hats with slits for eyes and midnight rides. It's just the way they look at us. Of course Boopy doesn't even notice. He says I'm being paranoid."

"Are you?"

"Maybe. But that doesn't mean I'm not right. I think paranoia is a very viable world view." She laughed, a well-pleased paranoid. Then she pointed at a tern emerging from the water with a tiny fish crosswise in its mouth. "Look at them *go*," she said. "They can do just exactly what they want."

"Well, we can too. If we want to, we can," he said, but as he said it he watched a tern perform a swift loop, a spin, and a long glide that was like falling—falling into grace. And he had to admit that the kind of freedom available to him suddenly seemed of the pocket-garden variety.

The pleasure of paranoia had faded from her face. "No. We can't," she said. "That's what's changed since we were children. Remember how easy everything was for us? You had all those toys, and I was the kindergarten prima ballerina." She made a face. "I really was. I was Dad's favorite, the one he'd play Ping-Pong with. Remember the little plays we put on? And I was always the star? And you were always the prince?"

"You were Princess Uggabooga," he said.

"That's right. I was Uggabooga from the word go. And you were Prince Robinson Crusoe."

"I was always Crusoe," he said happily.

"We were destined for great things," Tory said gravely.

"Oh, I don't know about great things. We were just kids. That was the great thing in itself."

"Then we had to grow up. And I discovered that, far from being able to do whatever I wanted, I couldn't really do anything at all."

"You must be nuts," he said. "You do everything well."

"No, not *very* well. I'm not fishing for compliments here, Egg. I can't do anything very well, but at least I can see who I am." She turned and put her hand on top of Egg's head, capping it; he could feel the palm against the bare skin of his bald spot, but he didn't dwell on that. He just felt thankful for the gesture. "I'm sorry," she said. "Your wife has just left you, and I sit here shooting my mouth off because I'm not Uggabooga any more. I just get blue when I end up doing things I don't want to do. Like yesterday. Boopy sent you off on a different path because he wanted to have sex on the beach. He loves it on the beach." Egg squeezed up his face as if he were hearing a graphic description of Montezuma's Revenge. "No, that wasn't the bad part," she said. "The bad part was that I wanted to walk with you. But I went ahead and left you alone because that's what he wanted."

"Why did you do it?" Egg asked, letting a little more anguish leak into his words than he'd intended to. His voice came perilously close to cracking.

"Well, I wanted to make him happy. I felt sorry for him. I always feel sorry for him."

"Is that any reason to make love to him?" he asked, but even as he did he answered his own question with a small, Eggian, mental Yes.

"Maybe not. But Boopy's right. That is what I'm here for." She smiled again. Though the smile was an unaccountable one, Egg, seeing it, felt that he was meeting an old friend on a railway platform. "That's my function," she said. "I'm Boopy's sex object. I'm a good object. I'm like a horse to him. Horses are graceful and lovely, but they're only born for someone to ride."

"I don't feel that way about horses," he said. He said it seriously, but Tory laughed.

"No," she said. "I guess I don't either. And I guess I'm being a little melodramatic. I do have another function. I'm Quammie's editor-in-residence. I'm not bad at it, and he certainly needs one. He disdains all forms of punctuation."

"Why stay?" he asked. "What do you get out of this?"

"What I get," Tory said, "is Boopy. I admire him. He's completely obsessed by his work. I really love people who get obsessed by things. I wish that just once I could lose myself in something. Anything. Flower arrangement. Double-crostics. That's one of your charms. I like the way you're obsessed by your wife. Of all things. Your *wife,* for heaven's sake."

"It's not so very odd," he said. He felt a trace of a blush rising; it had been a while since he'd thought of Jadis at all.

"It's not the least *bit* odd," she said. "It's totally ordinary. That's what's great about it. I mean, you have to run away from your wife when she's not even *there.*"

Was that what he was doing? He steered their talk away from these rocks. "How did you get involved with Professor Quammie in the first place?" he asked.

"Oh, he chased me. I thought he was a dear old goat. For a long time I wanted to keep my stupid insurance job in Massachusetts. I had been half a feminist once upon a time, and I couldn't imagine myself as Kept Woman. That was just pride. Finally I gave in. Because he wanted it so badly, the poor man. It probably wasn't what I wanted, but here I am. I'm not as unhappy as I used to think I should be. The sex is painless. I service Boopy. There's nothing nasty about it, Egg, you don't have to make faces. We all have our needs. And he does, you know, love me."

"Well," he said reluctantly, "I guess that's all anyone really needs."

"What is?"

"Love," Egg said.

"I just wish that were true," Tory said.

For a moment that was all either of them had to say. Their words brought on a sort of torpor, the way a film ending grimly, with everyone in the lifeboat dead, makes you feel more stiff on getting up than a simple triple wedding. Tory and Egg sat in silence, looking out over the river, the terns, the pelicans. Obese drops of rain began to fall on them, but they did not move.

Egg seemed to wake with a start. *"I don't know how the hell-he-can,"* he said. "That's the last line!" He said it as if the last line had eliminated all possibility of sadness.

"What last line?"

"I don't know how the hellhecan. That's it."

"Who? What are you talking about?"

"The pelican," he said. "I don't know how the hellhecan." It was all, he was trying to say, very simple.

Erica Jong

Fanny: Being the True History of the
Adventures of Fanny Hackabout-Jones

NOBLE Beginning; but then the Twig snapp'd! 'Twas no
Matter, for just at that Moment, there came a Knock upon
the Door, and, like a Conjurer at a Fair, I flipp'd the
Tablecloth o'er to its clean Side, secreted the charcoal Twig in my
Boot Top, and call'd:

"Enter!"

'Twas Polly with my roast Capon.

"If you please, Sir," said she.

"Thankee kindly, Polly," said I.

"Thank *you*, Sir," said she, flashing her Eyes at me.
Whereupon she tuckt a linen Napkin into my Shirt Front, taking
care to expose her fine, plump Bosom, just below my Nose, and I
receiv'd a most Pow'rful Odour of Attar of Roses, and honest

female Sweat, o'er and above the Odour of roast Capon: so much so that, 'twas fortunate I was not the Man I seem'd to be, for certainly the mingl'd Lusciousness of their entrancing Odours would have caus'd me to ravish Polly forthwith.

Instead, I made ready to ravish the Capon.

"Sit ye down, Lass," said I, "and talk to me whilst I have my Supper."

"Oh, Sir," said Polly, flutt'ring her Lashes. "I'm sure I daren't. The Landlord would surely turn me out o'Doors for such."

Now, our Polly was not one of those Slender Wenches who put one in mind of an Anatomist's Skeleton, and who would probably seem more like Broomstaffs than Women if one embraced 'em in Bed. No. She was, on the Contrary, so juicy and plump that she seem'd bursting thro' her tight Stays, e'en as the Flesh of the delicious roast Capon was bursting thro' its sewn Trussing. For a Moment, I almost fancied I was a Man and susceptible to her Charms. 'Twas all I could do to stop myself from thrusting an eager Hand into that Luscious Cleavage.

"Are you quite well, Sir?" she askt, bending o'er me with Solicitude (for, perhaps I lookt as queer as I felt). "Shall I cut your Capon for you?"

"Yes, Lass, please do so, for I have had a most wearying Journey and I can scarce find the Strength to do it myself."

She leant o'er me to pierce the juicy Flesh of the Capon; and, unable to contain myself any longer, I clapp'd my Mouth to the tender Valley betwixt the white Mountains of her Breasts and there insinuated my darting Tongue.

"Sir!" she cried with Alarm.

"A thousand Pardons!" I cried, sinking to my Knees, and kissing the Hem of her Garment. "A thousand Pardons. But I have this Day lost my own dear Mother and Grief hath left me distracted."

"Sir," she says, "I'll have you know I'm no Strumpet!" But i'faith, I could feel her softening a little at this Tale of Grief—which was, indeed, not so very far from being true.

I need hardly say, Belinda, that I was astonish'd by my own Behaviour, and yet, somehow I could not desist. Perhaps 'twas Grief that drove me to seduce a Maid when I was a mere Maid myself; perhaps 'twas something stranger still. Perhaps 'twas the wretched Influence of the God of the Witches (whom some call the Devil), or perhaps 'twas some long-lasting Result of the Flying Unguent, or yet perhaps some Madness brought on by the Horrors I had witness'd. Perhaps e'en 'twas my Muse's Way of showing me to feel both Man's and Woman's Passions. Or perhaps 'twas the mischievous Working of that Great Goddess in whom I only half believ'd.

At any Rate, I threw myself at Polly's Feet, and kiss'd her Hem, and then her Ankles, and then, since she made but little

Resistance, her Knees, and then, since she seem'd to sigh and invite it, her Thighs, and then, since she sat down upon a Chair and spread those Thighs (all the while protesting *No! No! No!* in the self-same Tone as *Yes! Yes! Yes!*), the sweet tender Ruby-red Cleft of her Sex itself, which lay expos'd to my View, since the Wench wore nothing at all 'neath her Shift and Petticoats.

Ah, the poor Capon lay deserted and steaming upon the Table (and 'neath that lay hidden my poor, scarce-started Epick), whilst I bent my Lips to Polly's tender Cleft and play'd Arpeggios with my own astonish'd Tongue. 'Twas salt as the Sea and tasted not unlike sweet Baby Oysters pluckt from the Bosom of the Deep.

"O Sir! O! O! O!" cries Polly, as I dart my Tongue in and out, inflam'd by her Words as well as her lovely ruby Slit. But, since by now her Petticoats are o'er my Head, I cannot fondle the twin Hillocks of her Breasts, but instead make free to stroke her milky Thighs, whilst her Petticoats make a sort of Tent in which I hide from all the Horrors of Mankind.

How warm and sweet it is inside a Petticoat! What Refuge from the Terrors of the World! What great Good Fortune to be born a Man and have such Refuge e'er within Grasp, within the warm World of a Woman's Hoop!

Gay Talese

Thy Neighbor's Wife

GOLDSTEIN was a regular of prostitutes in both the United States and Europe while in the Army, and it was not until he had been discharged and began attending Pace College on the G.I. Bill, in the winter of 1958, that he did not automatically expect to pay money for sex—and it was the first time, too, that he did not feel socially and intellectually inferior to nearly everyone around him. He had matured in the Army, had done considerable reading during many lonely nights in the barracks, and at Pace College he was two or three years older than most of his classmates, had traveled more than they had, and he enjoyed a certain status as a returning veteran. In addition to his success with his studies, he wrote for the campus newspaper, and worked each night after class as an apprentice photographer with his father at International News Photos. Having overcome the worst of his stuttering, he joined the college debating team, and was elected its captain.

But the realization that he was now more acceptable did not make him more accepting of other people; if anything his new self-confidence and status encouraged him to express more fully the hostility and frustration he had long felt. Now that his words could be understood he wanted to vengefully compensate for his many years of stifled rage and incoherent muttering that people had often mimicked; and if he should somehow achieve success in life, he knew that his greatest satisfaction would come from knowing that his old teachers and classmates in grade school had failed to perceive his winning potential.

Winning meant everything to Al Goldstein as a college debator, particularly when Pace was challenged by teams from the Ivy League, whose members he saw as socially privileged and rich, and therefore worthy of his scorn. In order to gain points against them Goldstein would do anything: He would falsify facts, would distort and lie in a dozen different ways—none of which disturbed his conscience because in his view Ivy Leaguers *deserved* to be lied to.

Soon, much of his churlishness was directed at Pace College itself. He began to feud with his professors, to write editorials denouncing campus policies, to rebel against the custom of students wearing a jacket and tie to class. As a twenty-one-year-old junior,

Goldstein had grown a beard and was recognized as the school's foremost beatnik; and as he neglected his textbooks for the novels of Kerouac and the poetry of Allen Ginsberg, his academic rating declined, although this was also due to the excessive amounts of time and energy he was devoting to an elusive, pretty co-ed who was on the debating team.

Since she represented his very first love experience, his ardor was as romantic as his expectations were naïve, especially since she was a sexually adventurous and popular young lady who had made it clear from the beginning that she did not intend to limit her social life exclusively to his nightly desires. Occasionally with his knowledge, and sometimes covertly, she dated other men—not consistently, but just often enough to keep Goldstein in a constant state of uncertainty and despair. His problem was that he could neither withdraw from her nor control her. She obsessed him physically. On nights when he was not in bed with her he masturbated to her image, seeing with maddening clarity her lean graceful figure and long, slender legs wrapped around the bodies of men he feared were more worthy than he was.

Though he was overweight, he had an aversion to overweight women; and despite the fact that his mother was large-breasted, or possibly because of it, Goldstein was lured by the smaller, firmer breasts of the sort that adorned the girl on the debating team; and while she had caused him much anguish since they had begun dating, reviving his old feelings of self-doubt, she also aroused his new combative spirit, his grim drive to conquer—she was, like the challenge of a debate itself, something he believed that he could finally win with his cunning mind, his quick mouth, and, in this particular instance, his cunnilingual tongue.

If there was a way to her heart, it was possibly through virtuoso performances upon her vulva, a conclusion he tentatively arrived at one night after she had gently pushed his head down between her legs and pronounced this to be her favorite pleasure. Prior to this, he had hardly ever heard of cunnilingus, and certainly never by that name. On the rare occasions when it had been referred to in the Army or in his Brooklyn neighborhood, it had prompted only vile and scrubby descriptions, the most polite of which was "muff-diving," and no self-respecting macho street hoodlum of his acquaintance had ever admitted to indulging in it. It was unmanly, if not unsanitary. It placed a man in a submissive role to a woman. It was primarily for perverts.

Indeed, after Goldstein had done research on the subject in the sex encyclopedias of various libraries, he discovered that cunnilingus, along with fellatio, was officially denied by the government as an obscene act, a form of sodomy, and it was illegal in most of the American states even when practiced in private by married couples.

In Connecticut the crime of oral sex could be punishable by a thirty-year jail term. In Ohio it was one to twenty years. In Georgia such a "crime against nature" could lead a practitioner to life imprisonment at hard labor—a penalty far more severe than having sex with animals, which in Georgia was punishable by only five years.

The laws against oral sex evolved of course from ecclesiastical law, which since the Middle Ages had determined these unprocreative acts to be unnatural, even though they had been natural enough to the multitudes who had practiced them since the earliest days of recorded civilization. Pictures showing people engaged in cunnilingus and fellatio could be found on Chinese scrolls dating back to 200 B.C., and also on ancient oriental rice bowls, perfume vases, and snuff bottles. Sculptured figures in erotic oral postures had appeared on early temples in India; and the first-century Roman satirist Juvenal referred often to cunnilingus and fellatio, suggesting that both were common during that time among heterosexuals as well as homosexuals. While the medieval church heavily penalized those who confessed to such pleasures, and created guilt within those who did not admit their sins, the oral predilection continued unabated for centuries in private, though it was rarely described and depicted openly except in forbidden art and literature, such as the eighteenth-century novel *Fanny Hill* and the much-censored work of Henry Miller.

Having read most of Miller's books, Goldstein was not only impressed with the author's vivid description of cunnilingus but was convinced that Miller himself greatly enjoyed bringing pleasure to a woman in this manner—and so did Al Goldstein, after much practice and encouragement from his young lady friend. When he had his head between her legs, and his tongue caressed her clitoris and vaginal lips, and his hands were firmly holding on to her buttocks and moving her at will, he sensed his power over her as he did at no other time. His tongue was a more potent weapon than his penis, or so it seemed to be during this period of his life; it was more reliable, tractable, responsive to his every command—his penis could be limp, unarousable, but his tongue was always capable of thrusting, curling, and whirling its way into her good graces; and as his mouth was upon her he was conscious not only of the luxuriance of her loins but also that he was making a literary connection with Henry Miller.

But when he was not in bed with her, she seemed indifferent to him, even more so after she began attending classes at night, and gradually during the fall of 1960 their relationship ended. Soon he found another girl, not quite so sophisticated but more attentive; and he cared for her less.

Oscar Wilde and Others

Teleny

IT was late at night, and I walked on without exactly knowing where my steps were taking me to. I had not to cross the water on my way home, what then made me do so? Anyhow, all at once I found myself standing in the very middle of the bridge, staring vacantly at the open space in front of me.

"The river like a silvery thoroughfare, parted the town in two. On either side huge shadowy houses rose out of the mist; blurred domes, dim towers, vaporous and gigantic spires soared, quivering, up to the clouds, and faded away in the fog.

"Underneath I could perceive the sheen of the cold, bleak, and bickering river, flowing faster and faster, as if fretful at not being able to outdo itself in its own speed, chafing against the arches that stopped it, curling in tiny breakers, and whirling away in angry eddies, whilst the dark pillars shed patches of ink-black shade on the glittering and shivering stream.

"As I looked upon these dancing, restless shadows, I saw a myriad of fiery, snake-like elves gliding to and fro through them, winking and beckoning to me as they twirled and they rolled, luring me down to rest in those Lethean waters.

"They were right. Rest must be found below those dark arches, on the soft, slushy sand of that swirling river.

"How deep and fathomless those waters seemed! Veiled as they were by the mist, they had all the attraction of the abyss. Why should I not seek there that balm of forgetfulness which alone could ease my aching head, could calm my burning breast?

"Why?

"Was it because the Almighty had fixed His canon against self-slaughter?

"How, when, and where?"

"With His fiery finger, when He made that *coup de théâtre* on Mount Sinai?

"If so, why was He tempting my beyond my strength?

"Would any father induce a beloved child to disobey him, simply to have the pleasure of chastising him afterwards? Would any man deflower his own daughter, not out of lust, but only to taunt her with her incontinence? Surely, if such a man ever lived, he was after Jehovah's own image.

"No, life is only worth living as long as it is pleasant. To me, just then, it was a burden. The passion I had tried to stifle, and which was merely smouldering, had burst out with renewed strength, entirely mastering me. That crime could therefore only be overcome by another. In my case suicide was not only allowable, but laudable—nay, heroic.

"What did the Gospel say? 'If thine eye . . . .' and so forth.

"All these thoughts whirled through my mind like little fiery snakes. Before me in the mist, Teleny—like a vaporous angel of light—seemed to be quietly gazing at me with his deep, sad, and thoughtful eyes; below, the rushing waters had for me a syren's sweet, enticing voice.

"I felt my brain reeling. I was losing my senses. I cursed this beautiful world of ours—this paradise, that man has turned into hell. I cursed this narrow-minded society of ours, that only thrives upon hypocrisy. I cursed our blighting religion, that lays its veto upon all the pleasures of the senses.

"I was already climbing on the parapet, decided to seek forget-fulness in those Stygian waters, when two strong arms clasped me tightly and held me fast."

"It was Teleny?"

"It was."

"'Camille, my love, my soul, are you mad?' said he, in a stifled, panting voice.

"Was I dreaming—was it he? Teleny? Was he my guardian angel or a tempting demon? Had I gone quite mad?

"All these thoughts chased one another, and left me bewildered. Still, after a moment, I understood that I was neither mad nor dreaming. It was Teleny in flesh and blood, for I felt him against me as we were closely clasped in each other's arms. I had wakened to life from a horrible nightmare.

"The strain my nerves had undergone, and the utter faintness that followed, together with his powerful embrace, made me feel as if our two bodies clinging closely together had amalgamated or melted into a single one.

"A most peculiar sensation came over me at this moment. As my hands wandered over his head, his neck, his shoulders, his arms, I could not feel him at all; in fact, it seemed to me as if I were touching my own body. Our burning foreheads were pressed against each other, and his swollen and throbbing veins seemed my own fluttering pulses.

"Instinctively, and without seeking each other, our mouths united by a common consent. We did not kiss, but our breath gave life to our two beings.

"I remained vaguely unconscious for some time, feeling my strength ebb slowly away, leaving but vitality enough to know that I was yet alive.

"All at once I felt a mighty shock from head to foot; there was a reflux from the heart to the brain. Every nerve in my body was tingling; all my skin seemed pricked with the points of sharp needles. Our mouths which had withdrawn now clung again to each other with newly-awakened lust. Our lips—clearly seeking to engraft themselves together—pressed and rubbed with such passionate strength that the blood began to ooze from them—nay, it seemed as if this fluid, rushing up from our two hearts, was bent upon mingling together to celebrate in that auspicious moment the old hymeneal rites of nations—the marriage of two bodies, not by the communion of emblematic wine but of blood itself.

"We thus remained for some time in a state of overpowering delirium, feeling every instant, a more rapturous, maddening pleasure in each other's kisses, which kept goading us on to madness by increasing that heat which they could not allay, and by stimulating that hunger they could not appease.

"The very quintessence of love was in these kisses. All that was excellent in us—the essential part of our beings—kept rising and evaporating from our lips like the fumes of an ethereal, intoxicating, ambrosial fluid.

"Nature, hushed and silent, seemed to hold her breath to look upon us, for such ecstasy of bliss had seldom, if ever, been felt here below. I was subdued, prostrated, shattered. The earth was spinning round me, sinking under my feet. I had no longer strength enough to stand. I felt sick and faint. Was I dying? If so, death must be the happiest moment of our life, for such rapturous joy could never be felt again.

"How long did I remain senseless? I cannot tell. All I know is that I awoke in the midst of a whirlwind, hearing the rushing of waters around me. Little by little I came back to consciousness. I tried to free myself from his grasp.

" 'Leave me! Leave me alone! Why did you not let me die? This world is hateful to me, why should I drag on a life I loathe?'

" 'Why? For my sake.' Thereupon, he whispered softly, in that unknown tongue of his, some magic words which seemed to sink into my soul. Then he added, 'Nature has formed us for each other; why withstand her? I can only find happiness in your love, and in your's alone; it is not only part of my heart but my soul that panteth for your's.'

"With an effort of my whole being I pushed him away from me, and staggered back.

" 'No, no!' I cried, 'do not tempt me beyond my strength; let me rather die.'

" 'Thy will be done, but we shall die together, so that at least in death we may not be parted. There is an after-life, we may then, at least, cleave to one another like Dante's Francesca and her lover Paulo. Here,' said he, unwinding a silken scarf that he wore round his waist, 'let us bind ourselves closely together, and leap into the flood.'

"I looked at him, and shuddered. So young, so beautiful, and I was thus to murder him! The vision of Antinoüs as I had seen it the first time he played appeared before me.

"He had tied the scarf tightly round his waist, and he was about to pass it around me.

" 'Come.'

"The die was cast. I had not the right to accept such a sacrifice from him.

" 'No,' quoth I, 'let us live.'

" 'Live,' added he, 'and then?'

"He did not speak for some moments, as if waiting for a reply to that question which had not been framed in words. In answer to his mute appeal I stretched out my hands towards him. He—as if frightened that I should escape him—hugged me tightly with all the strength of irrepressible desire.

" 'I love you!' he whispered, 'I love you madly! I cannot live without you any longer.'

" 'Nor can I,' said I, faintly; 'I have struggled against my passion in vain, and now I yield to it, not tamely, but eagerly, gladly. I am your's, Teleny! Happy to be your's, your's forever and your's alone!'

"For all answer there was a stifled hoarse cry from his inner-most breast; his eyes were lighted up with a flash of fire; his craving amounted to rage; it was that of the wild beast seizing his prey; that of the lonely male finding at last a mate. Still his intense eagerness was more than that; it was also a soul issuing forth to meet another soul. It was a longing of the senses, and a mad intoxication of the brain.

"Could this burning, unquenchable fire that consumed our bodies be called lust? We clung as hungrily to one another as the famished animal does when it fastens on the food it devours; and as we kissed each other with ever-increasing greed, my fingers were feeling his curly hair, or paddling the soft skin of his neck. Our legs being clasped together, his phallus, in strong erection, was rubbing against mine no less stiff and stark. We were, however, always shifting our position, so as to get every part of our bodies in as close a contact as possible; and thus feeling, clasping, hugging, kissing, and biting each other, we must have looked, on that bridge amidst the thickening fog, like two damned souls suffering eternal torment.

"The hand of Time had stopped; and I think we should have continued goading each other in our mad desire until we had quite lost our senses—for we were both on the verge of madness—had we not been stopped by a trifling incident.

"A belated cab—wearied with the day's toil—was slowly

trudging its way homeward. The driver was sleeping on his box; the poor, broken-down jade, with its head drooping almost between its knees, was likewise slumbering—dreaming, perhaps of unbroken rest, of new-mown hay, of the fresh and flowery pastures of its youth; even the slow rumbling of the wheels had a sleepy, purring, snoring sound in its irksome sameness.

" 'Come home with me,' said Teleny, in a low, nervous, and trembling voice; 'come and sleep with me,' added he, in the soft, hushed, and pleading tone of the lover who would fain be understood without words.

"I pressed his hands for all answer.

" 'Will you come?'

" 'Yes,' I whispered, almost inaudibly.

"This low, hardly-articulate sound was the hot breath of vehement desire; this lisped monosyllable was the willing consent to his eagerest wish.

"Then he hailed the passing cab, but it was some moments before the driver could be awakened and made to understand what we wanted of him.

"As I stepped into the vehicle, my first thought was that in a few minutes Teleny would belong to me. This thought acted upon my nerves as an electric current, making me shiver from head to foot.

"My lips had to articulate the words, 'Teleny will be mine,' for me to believe it. He seemed to hear the noiseless movement of my lips, for he clasped my head between his hands, and kissed me again and again.

"Then, as if feeling a pang of remorse—'You do not repent, do you?' he asked.

" 'How can I?'

" 'And you will be mine—mine alone?'

" 'I never was any other man's, nor ever shall be.'

" 'You will love me for ever?'

" 'And ever.'

" 'This will be our oath and act of possession,' added he.

"Thereupon he put his arms around me and clasped me to his breast. I entwined my arms round him. By the glimmering, dim light of the cab-lamps I saw his eyes kindle with the fire of madness. His lips—parched with the thirst of his long-suppressed desire, with the pent-up craving of possession—pouted towards mine with a painful expression of dull suffering. We were again sucking up each other's being in a kiss—a kiss more intense, if possible, than the former one. What a kiss that was!

"The flesh, the blood, the brain, and that undefined subtler part of our being seemed all to melt together in an ineffable embrace.

"A kiss is something more than the first sensual contact of two bodies; it is the breathing forth of two enamoured souls.

"But a criminal kiss long withstood and fought against, and therefore long yearned after, is beyond this; it is as luscious as forbidden fruit; it is a glowing coal set upon the lips, a fiery brand that burns deep, and changes the blood into molten lead or scalding quicksilver.

"Teleny's kiss was really galvanic, for I could taste its sapidity upon my palate. Was an oath needed, when we had given ourselves to one another with such a kiss? An oath is a lip-promise which can be, and is, often forgotten. Such a kiss follows you to the grave.

"Whilst our lips clung together, his hand slowly, imperceptibly, unbuttoned my trousers, and stealthily slipped within the aperture, turning every obstacle in its way instinctively aside, then it lay hold of my hard, stiff, and aching phallus which was glowing like a burning coal.

"This grasp was as soft as a child's, as expert as a whore's, as strong as a fencer's. He had hardly touched me than I remembered the Countess's words.

"Some people, as we all know, are more magnetic than others. Moreover, whilst some attract, others repel us. Teleny had—for me, at least—a supple, mesmeric, pleasure-giving fluid in his fingers. Nay, the simple contact of his skin thrilled me with delight.

"My own hand hesitantly followed the lead his had given, and I must confess the pleasure I felt in paddling him was really delightful.

"Our fingers hardly moved the skin of the penis; but our nerves were so strained, our excitement had reached such a pitch, and the seminal ducts were so full, that we felt them overflowing. There was, for a moment, an intense pain, somewhere about the root of the penis—or rather, within the very core and centre of the reins, after which the sap of life began to move slowly, slowly, from within the seminal glands; it mounted up the bulb of the urethra, and up the narrow column, somewhat like mercury within the tube of a thermometer—or rather, like the scalding and scathing lava within the crater of a volcano.

"It finally reached the apex; then the slit gaped, the tiny lips parted, and the pearly, creamy, viscous fluid oozed out—not all at once in a gushing jet, but at intervals, and in huge, burning tears.

"At every drop that escaped out of the body, a creepy almost unbearable feeling started from the tips of the fingers, from the ends of the toes, especially from the innermost cells of the brain; the marrow in the spine and within all the bones seemed to melt; and when the different currents—either coursing with the blood or running rapidly up the nervous fibres—met within the phallus (that small instrument made out of muscles and blood-vessels) a tremendous shock took place; a convulsion which annihilated both mind and matter, a quivering delight which everyone has felt, to a greater or lesser degree—often a thrill almost too intense to be pleasurable.

"Pressed against each other, all we could do was to try and smother our groans as the fiery drops slowly followed one another.

"The prostration which followed the excessive strain of the nerves had set in, when the carriage stopped before the door of Teleny's house—that door at which I had madly struck with my fist a short time before.

"We dragged ourselves wearily out of the carriage, but hardly had the portal shut itself upon us than we were again kissing and fondling each other with renewed energy.

"After some moments, feeling that our desire was too powerful to be withstood any longer—'Come,' said he, 'why should we linger any longer, and waste precious time here in the darkness and in the cold?'

" 'Is it dark and is it cold?' was my reply.

"He kissed me fondly.

" 'In the gloom you are my light; in the cold you are my fire; the frozen wastes of the pole would be a Garden of Eden for me, if you were there,' I continued.

"We then groped our way upstairs in the dark, for I would not allow him to light a wax match. I therefore went along, stumbling against him; not that I could not see, but because I was intoxicated with mad desire as a drunken man is with wine.

"Soon we were in his apartment. When we found ourselves in the small, dimly-lighted antechamber, he opened his arms and stretched them out towards me.

" 'Welcome!' said he. 'May this home be ever thine.' Then he added, in a low tone, in that unknown, musical tongue, 'My body hungereth for thee, soul of my soul, life of my life!'

"He had barely finished these words before we were lovingly caressing each other.

"After thus fondling each other for a few moments—'Do you know,' said he, 'that I have been expecting you today?'

" 'Expecting me?'

" 'Yes, I knew that sooner or later you would be mine. Moreover, I felt that you would be coming today.'

" 'How so?'

" 'I had a presentiment.'

" 'And had I not come?'

" 'I should have done what you were going to do when I met you, for life without you would have been unbearable.'

" 'What! drowned yourself?'

" 'No, not exactly: the river is too cold and bleak, I am too much of a Sybarite for that. No, I should simply have put myself to sleep—the eternal slumber of death, dreaming of you, in this room prepared to receive you, and where no man has ever set his foot.'

"Saying these words he opened the door of [a] small chamber, and ushered me into it. A strong, overpowering smell of white heliotrope first greeted my nostrils.

"It was a most peculiar room, the walls of which were covered over with some warm, white, soft, quilted stuff, studded all over with frosted silver buttons; the floor was covered with the curly white fleece of young lambs; in the middle of the apartment stood a capacious couch, on which was thrown the skin of a huge polar bear. Over this single piece of furniture, an old silver lamp—evidently from some Byzantine church or some Eastern synagogue—shed a pale glimmering light, sufficient, however, to light up the dazzling whiteness of this temple of Priapus whose votaries we were.

" 'I know,' said he, as he dragged me in, 'I know that white is your favourite color, that it suits your dark complexion, so it has been fitted up for you and you alone. No other mortal shall ever set his foot in it.'

"Uttering these words, he in a trice stripped me deftly of all my clothes—for I was in his hands like a slumbering child, or a man in a trance.

"In an instant I was not only stark naked, but stretched on the bear-skin, whilst he, standing in front of me, was gloating upon me with famished eyes.

"I felt his glances greedily fall everywhere; they sank in my brain, and my head began to swim; they pierced through my heart, whipping my blood up, making it flow quicker and hotter through all the arteries; they darted within my veins, and Priapus unhooded itself and lifted up its head violently so that all the tangled web of veins in its body seemed ready to burst.

"Then he felt me with his hands everywhere, after which he began to press his lips on every part of my body, showering kisses on my breast, my arms, my legs, my thighs, and then, when he had reached my middle parts, he pressed his face rapturously on the thick and curly hair that grows there so plentifully.

"He shivered with delight as he felt the crisp locks upon his cheek and neck; then, taking hold of my phallus, he pressed his lips upon it. That seemed to electrify him; and then the tip and afterwards the whole glans disappeared within his mouth.

"As it did so, I could hardly keep quiet. I clasped within my hands his curly and scented head; a shiver ran through my whole body; all my nerves were on edge; the sensation was so keen that it almost maddened me.

"Then the whole column was in his mouth, the tip was touching his palate; his tongue, flattened or thickened, tickling me everywhere. Now I was sucked greedily, then nibbled or bitten. I screamed, I called on him to stop. I could not bear such intensity any longer; it was killing me. If it had lasted but a trice longer I should have lost my senses. He was deaf and ruthless to my entreaties. Flashes of lightning seemed to be passing before my eyes; a torrent of fire was coursing through my body.

" 'Enough—stop, enough!' I groaned.

"My nerves were extended; a thrill came over me; the soles of my feet seemed to have been drilled through. I writhed; I was convulsed.

"One of his hands which had been caressing my testicles slipped under my bum—a finger was slipped in the hole. I seemed to be a man in front, a woman behind, for the pleasure I felt either way.

"My trepidation had reached its climax. My brain reeled; my body melted; the burning milk of life was again mounting up, like a sap of fire; my bubbling blood mounted up to my brain, maddening me. I was exhausted; I fainted with pleasure; I fell upon him—a lifeless mass!

"In a few minutes I was myself again—eager to take his place, and to return the caresses I had just received.

"I tore the clothes from his body, so that he was speedily as naked as I was. What a pleasure it was to feel his skin against mine from head to foot! Moreover, the delight I had just felt had only increased my eagerness, so that, after clasping each other and wrestling together for a few moments, we both rolled on the floor, twisting, and rubbing, and crawling, and writhing, like two heated cats exciting each other into a paroxysm of rage.

"But my lips were eager to taste his phallus—an organ which might have served as a model for the huge idol in the temple of Priapus, or over the doors of the Pompeian brothels, only that at the sight of this wingless god most men would have—as many did— discarded women for the love of their fellow-men. It was big without having the proportion of an ass's; it was thick and rounded, though slightly tapering; the glans—a fruit of flesh and blood, like a small apricot—looked pulpy, round and appetizing.

"I feasted my hungry eyes upon it; I handled it; I kissed it; I felt its soft glossy skin upon my lip; it moved with an inward motion of its own, as I did so. My tongue then deftly tickled the tip, trying to dart itself between those tiny rosy lips that, bulged out with love, opened and spattered a tiny drop of sparkling dew. I licked the fore-skin, then sucked the whole of it, pumping it greedily. He moved it vertically whilst I tried to clasp it tightly with my lips; he thrust it further every time, and touched my palate; it almost reached my throat, and I felt it quivering with a life of its own; I moved quicker, quicker, quicker. He clasped my head furiously; all his nerves were throbbing.

" 'Your mouth is burning—you are sucking out my very brain! Stop, stop! my whole body is aglow! I can't—any more! I can't—it is too much!'

"He grasped my head tightly to make me stop, but I pressed his phallus tightly with my lips, my cheeks, my tongue; my movements were more and more rapid, so that after a few strokes I felt him shudder from head to foot, as if seized by a fit of giddiness. He sighed, he groaned, he screamed. A jet of warm, soapy, acrid liquid filled my mouth. His head reeled; the pleasure he felt was so sharp that it verged upon pain.

" 'Stop, stop!' he moaned faintly, shutting his eyes and panting.

"I, however, was maddened by the idea that he was not truly mine, that I was drinking down the fiery foaming sap of his body, the real elixir of life.

"His arms for a moment clasped me convulsively. A rigidity then came over him; he was shattered by such an excess of wantonness.

"I myself felt almost as much as he did, for in my fury I sucked him eagerly, greedily, and thus provoked an abundant ejaculation; and at the same time small drops of the same fluid which I was receiving in me, coursed slowly, painfully, out of my body. As this happened, our nerves relaxed and we fell exhausted upon one another.

"A short space of rest—I cannot tell how long, intensity not being measured by Time's sedate pace—and then I felt his nerveless penis re-awaken from its sleep, and press against my face; it was evidently trying to find my mouth, just like a greedy but glutted baby even in its sleep holds firm the nipple of its mother's breast simply for the pleasure of having it in its mouth.

"I pressed my mouth upon it, and, like a young cock awakened at early dawn stretches forth its neck and crows lustily, it thrust its head towards my warm, pouted lips.

"As soon as I had it in my mouth, Teleny wheeled himself around, and placed himself in the same position that I was to him; that is, his mouth was at the height of my middle part, only with the difference that I was on my back and he was over me.

"He began to kiss my rod; he played with the bushy hair that grew around it; he patted my buttocks, and, especially, he caressed my testicles with a knack all his own that filled me with unutterable delight.

"His hands so increased the pleasure his mouth and his own phallus were giving me that I was soon beyond myself with excitement.

"Our two bodies were one mass of quivering sensuality; and although we were both increasing the rapidity of our movements, still we were so maddened with lust that in that tension of the nerves the seminal glands refused to do their work.

"We laboured on in vain. My reason all at once left me; the parched blood within me vainly tried to ooze out, and it seemed to swirl in my injected eyes; it tingled in my ears. I was in a paroxysm of erotic rage—in a paroxysm of mad delirium.

"My brain seemed trepanned, my spine sawn in two. Nevertheless I sucked his phallus quicker and quicker; I drew it like a teat; I tried to drain it; and I felt him palpitate, quiver, shudder. All at once the gates of the sperm were opened, and from hellish fires we were uplifted, amidst a shower of burning sparks, into a delightfully calm and ambrosial Olympus.

"After a few moments' rest I uplifted myself on my elbow, and delighted my eyes with my lover's fascinating beauty. He was a very model of carnal comeliness; his chest was broad and strong, his arms rounded; in fact, I have never seen such a vigorous and at the same time agile frame; for not only was there not the slightest fat but not even the least superfluous flesh about him. He was all nerve, muscle, and sinew. It was his well-knit and supple joints that gave him the free, easy, and graceful motion so characteristic of the Felidæ, of which he had also the flexibility, for when he clasped himself to you he seemed to entwine himself around you like a snake. Moreover, his skin was of a pearly almost iridescent whiteness, whilst the hair on the different parts of his body except the head was quite black.

"Teleny opened his eyes, stretched out his arms towards me, took hold of my hand, kissed, and then bit me on the nape of the neck; then he showered a number of kisses all along my back, which, following one another in quick succession, seemed like a rain of rose-leaves falling from some full-blown flower.

"Then he reached the two fleshy lobes which he pressed open with his hands, and darted his tongue in that hole where a little while before he had thrust his finger. This likewise was for me a new and thrilling sensation.

"This done, he rose and stretched forth his hand to lift me up.

" 'Now,' said he, 'let us go in the next room, and see if we can find something to eat; for I think we really require some food, though, perhaps, a bath would not be amiss before we sit down to supper. Should you like to have one?'

" 'It might put you to inconvenience.'

"For all answer he ushered me into a kind of cell, all filled with ferns and feathery palms, that—as he shewed me—received during the day the rays of the sun from a skylight overhead.

" 'This is a kind of make-shift for a hot-house and a bath-room, which every habitable dwelling ought to have. I am too poor to have either, still this hole is big enough for my ablutions, and my plants seem to thrive pretty well in this warm and damp atmosphere.'

" 'But it's a princely bath-room!'

" 'No, no!' said he, smiling; 'it's an artist's bath-room.'

"We at once plunged into the warm water, scented, with essence of heliotrope; and it was so pleasant to rest there locked in each other's arms after our last excesses.

" 'I could stay here all night,' he mused, 'it is so delightful to handle you in this warm water. But you must be famished, so we had better go and get something to satisfy the inward cravings.'

"We got out, and wrapped ourselves up for a moment with hot *peignoirs* of Turkish towelling.

" 'Come,' said he, 'let me lead you to the dining-room.'

"I stood hesitating, looking first at my nakedness, then upon his. He smiled, and kissed me.

" 'You don't feel cold, do you?'

" 'No, but—'

" 'Well, then, don't be afraid; there is no one in the house. Everyone is asleep on the other flats, and besides, every window is tightly shut, and all the curtains are down.'

"He dragged me with him into a neighbouring room all covered with thick, soft, and silky carpets, the prevailing tone of which was dull Turkish red.

"In the centre of this apartment hung a curiously-wrought, starshaped lamp, which the faithful—even now-a-days—light on Friday eve.

"We sat down on a soft-cushioned divan, in front of one of those ebony Arab tables all inlaid with coloured ivory and iridescent mother-of-pearl.

" 'I cannot give you a banquet, although I expected you; still, there is enough to satisfy your hunger, I hope.'

"There were some luscious Cancale oysters—few, but of an immense size; a dusty bottle of Sauternes, then a *pâté de foie gras* highly scented with Perigord truffles; a partridge, with *paprika* or Hungarian curry, and a salad made out of a huge Piedmont truffle, as thinly sliced as shavings, and a bottle of exquisite dry sherry.

"All these delicacies were served in dainty blue old Delft and Savona ware, for he had already heard of my hobby for old majolica.

"Then came a dish of Seville oranges, bananas, and pineapples, flavoured with Maraschino and covered with sifted sugar. It was a savoury, tasty, tart and sweet medley, combining together the flavour and perfume of all these delicious fruits.

"After having washed it down with a bottle of sparkling champagne, we then sipped some tiny cups of fragrant and scalding Mocha coffee; then he lighted a narghilè, or Turkish water pipe, and we puffed at intervals the odorous Latakiah, inhaling it with our ever-hungry kisses from each other's mouths.

"The fumes of the smoke and those of the wine rose up to our heads, and in our re-awakened sensuality we soon had between our lips a far more fleshy mouth-piece than the amber one of the Turkish pipe.

"Our heads were again soon lost between each other's thighs. We had once more but one body between us, juggling with one another, ever seeking new caresses, new sensations, a sharper and more inebriating kind of lewdness, in our anxiety not only to enjoy ourselves but to make the other one feel. We were, therefore, very soon the prey of a blasting lust, and only some inarticulate sounds expressed the climax of our voluptuous state, until, more dead than alive, we fell upon each other—a mingled mass of shivering flesh."

Laura Chester

Correspondence

I WANT you to be reading this, as I make love to your cock. I want you to be standing there, reading this, looking down at the top of my head, engaged in the act of loving you, maybe looking up myself, to smile through half-closed eyes, only to sink again, into the pleasure of mouthing you, and I can feel you getting harder, wanting to push it in a little deeper, and I am getting myself aroused, reaching up to touch from your chest, expanded, down with curving nails, to where I can hold the stalk, and lick the tip and kiss your tightening balls. I want you to be engaged inside my orifice. I want you to feel me feel the meat of your buttocks, as you plunge, withdraw and plunge, as you collect my hair and groan—I want it to be so good you want to free yourself in my mouth. I want you to fold this poem as if you can't stand to stand uncertain anymore, but have to let it go, allow—And let the paper fall, just as I make (imaginary) love to you—Real in the mail.

Charles Simmons

Powdered Eggs

I WENT to the post office this morning to look for mail. There was none, you bastard, and when I came out into the brilliant sunlight I felt dizzy. It was coolish, so it wasn't the weather, but I suddenly sensed that I was three thousand miles away. What I was away from I don't know, but it was three thousand miles, and I felt like a child that had been lost or abandoned by his parents. I went back into the post office, and the clerk smiled at me. Smiling wops, I thought, but for his benefit I slapped my pocket as if I had forgotten something, smiled back and left. It got worse, the world was spinning under me—spinning as it really does—but now I could feel it. I thought I might fall over, so I tried to walk, and luckily, by going slowly and keeping my legs apart I got to the church, an ancient beat-up building no bigger than a chapel. An old guy, a layman, was fussing around the altar. I asked him for the priest. Whatever priest is in Italian, I just said Priest, and he came back with a skinny dark man who looked annoyed but willing to listen. I went down on my knees right in the center aisle. Any Irish cleric would have played it like Italian opera and become a small Jesus, but this guy rubbed one hand over his forehead and with the other picked me up by the elbow and pushed me into a pew. He sat down beside me and by turning his profile adopted the manner of the confessor. The sexton came close to observe the proceedings. I didn't care, it seemed like it should be a group effort anyway. Do you speak English, Father, I said to the priest. He nodded, but obviously he didn't. Do you speak English, I said, turning to the sexton. He nodded too. OK, bless me, Father, I don't believe in what you represent, but I believe in you. Do you understand that? He nodded. I think the Church is a lot of shit, really, but it has a piece of me marked out. He nodded. I wanted to confess that I have been inadequate in my life, I haven't produced what the world has required of me, not what my father required, or my mother, or my employer, or my friends, or what I have required of myself, even. This is a terrible sin, do you understand? He nodded. Are you sure you don't understand English, I said to the sexton, who was surprised at being addressed again and nodded solemnly in response. Maybe most of all I didn't produce what our own organization required of me, Father. In defense of myself I can say that I tried very hard, but I think that different groups and people asked contradictory things of me. He nodded. I did satisfy my schools, though, and my new doctor thinks I'm all right and will be all right, and some of my friends do, too, I think. I say this in the spirit of evidence, not as justification, do you understand? And he nodded. I've done certain things, which have made me a certain thing. I mean that a lot of my future is already determined, so that I can't make any sweeping promises, and that's all I have to say. He turned his serious dark face to me as if to make sure that I was done, and I thought as I looked at him that this was a whore of the soul, a wonderful whore of the soul, because he was going to give me what I wanted. I want you to forgive me to the extent that you can, for all my inadequacies, and I held up my hands to indicate that was that. He moved right into Latin, which sounded like Italian, but I heard the words Ego te absolvo, and this was a great giving, I can tell you, because the guy didn't know what I had said, I could have come from Rome after killing the Pope, but Ego te absolvo, he said, and he looked at me again to make sure there was nothing else. Grazie, I said. He nodded a final time, got up and went whence he came. The sexton returned to his dusting or whatever, and out in the sun it was gone, I had my earth legs back. And more. The colors of the sky and the road and the faded stones and the great quiet lake, which I could see down the side streets, looked deep and rich. I felt more like a child than at any time since

I was a child. Jesus, I was hungry and horny, I wanted to write books and play tennis and see movies, only all at once, so since they were serving at the hotel, I settled for lunch of soup and fish and salad and vino blanco. During previous meals I had noticed that a Hollandaise lady, of about thirty years, was also seated alone. Our eyes had met six, seven times, and after Prudence left I had secreted her image in my head like a gumdrop under the gum. Our eyes met again, but there was a big rosy famishedness about her that had and continued to put me off. Perhaps at dinner I would ask the captain to see if I could join her, but now I wanted to consolidate my new position. I would eat, go up for a siesta, swim in the afternoon, dress sweet for dinner and see. When I got to my room, however, the chambermaiden, a tiny girl and fair, was tidying. We, too, had noticed one another. As I came in she made to leave, but I smiled the smile of Italy and motioned her to go on. I flopped on the bed and watched. She seemed to be doing her work so slowly. Was I falling asleep, or was she lingering? Time almost stopped, and I felt I was in a crib, this was my nursemaid I was three thousand miles away, wasn't the chambermaiden preparing something nice for me in consolation? A bottle? Or would she put a blanket on me? Then suddenly she seemed finished. But she had not done the nice thing. My eyes were half closed, I motioned to her with my hand. The childish part of me knew that she would come, the adult part that she wouldn't. But she did, she came to the foot of the bed. I must do something else to keep her. If I go on lying here she will leave. I had to rouse myself. Like lifting many pounds I sat up. I must do still more. I shinnied down to the foot of the bed. Still more. I slid onto my knees. My head came between her breasts, she was that tiny. So I sat back on my heels. I put my arms around her legs and pressed my face into her dress. I rubbed my nose and forehead against her and could feel the hair through her clothes. Was I frightening her? I was afraid to look up to find out. I so wanted her to stay, and by being a child, I thought, I could keep her. She wouldn't desert a child. I heard the hairs scratching against one another against the skirt as I rubbed with my forehead. Hello, coozie, I said. The chambermaiden said something irrelevant far above me. I'm talking to the coozie, I said, I'll talk to you later. You up there, before you fly away like a bird or pull away like a woman, I first want to say something to the coozie. I want to say that you are my one true friend, who never did me any wrong, and however your owner feels about me up there, I know you like me, don't you, crazy crack, don't you, crazy follicles? Crazy bone, I love you, I said, and put my hands and arms under the back of her skirt. She had no pants on. Her little white blouse had long sleeves and a high bodice, but she had no pants on. Her tiny ass was taut to my touch, but I loved it so much that it finally relaxed. I'm going to take a picture, I said, you won't be frightened if I take a picture, will you? And her mouth said something in Italian, so I pulled the front of her skirt over my head and closed my eyes to complete the darkness. I pressed my nose between her legs and up against the bone, her hair was in my eyes. I nuzzled her like a dog. She spread her feet slightly and in my darkness I licked her, crouching down, bending my head back. I could hear her voice, saying words or making sounds, but it was out in the light far away. I was with my friend, and whatever was going on in the owner's head didn't matter so long as she didn't take my friend away. Well, I drank my chambermaiden, I ate the rose. Her legs were shaking so, I thought she'd fall, and finally she put her hands under my arms and lifted me up. It was like growing from infancy, and she was a tiny girl again, her eyes on level with my chest. I bent down and kissed her, and she tasted herself in my mouth. We both came together. She couldn't stay long, which struck me as ironic. Here I was, a guest, every wish realized, and my chambermaiden, whom I would so dearly have wished to keep with me, had to run off to change towels. Her name is Ermina, she lives here year around with Mommie and Daddie, two brothers and two sisters. The family has been in Bardolino for as many generations as memory serves. Daddie was a fisherman until recent years and now works for one or another of the hotels as handyman. Her brothers are in the Italian Navy sailing on the small fleet that plies the ports of Largo di Garda. She says they are very handsome, which I do not doubt, Italy puts the flower of its youth into the transportation services. Her sisters are younger than she and still go to school. Ermina works for only five months a year, since Bardolino is a warm-weather resort. The rest of the year she helps her mother, at what I couldn't make out with my pocket dictionary. I wanted to discover other things, though. Whether she plans to stay in Bardolino, and why she went to bed with me, but we couldn't get across to one another. She's coming back after dinner. This afternoon I'm going to the dock for a late swim, while she helps out in the kitchen. Jesus. She explained with the help of my watch that she'll have to leave by nine-thirty or Daddie will be angry. He doesn't mind her working, she said, but he distrusts the northern Europeans who come to Bardolino in the fall and summer—the French, Dutch, English, and especially the Germans. No one who distrusts the Germans can be all bad, I thought. What about the Americans, I said. Everybody likes the Americans, she said.

Cerridwen Fallingstar

The Heart of the Fire

LIKE every loss of innocence, it started innocently enough. We were twelve, brash hooligans wild as lynx or lark or the unpredictable spring storms. We were still not above stealing the horse-shoes over someone's barn or tying elf-locks in their horses' manes and tails. We could be thoughtful, leaving bunches of flowers on people's doorsteps. On the other hand, we were just as likely to leave a basket of snails. Early April, the ground already thawing. Annie's cat had just had kittens.

Up in the loft, tickling each other into hysteria rolling off the blanket into the hay, yellow prickles in our hair, "Ow! Stop yer silliness!" giggles snickers snorts horsey smells in our noses. "You be the kitten an' I'll be Tawny," you say. "If yer the mumcat where are yer teats?" Russet kitten I become, pawing through your clothes in search of milk. I find your slight breast and latch on. Your turn to cry out and cuff me. "Ow, damn kitten, I think yer father was a robber lynx! Coory doon bairn 'tis time fer yer bath." I make no protest as she undresses me. We've slept and played naked together often, to both our mothers' distress. "Gypsy brat!" her mother would screech at her when Annie palmed the bannocks or rifled her purse, or cut up her clothes into costumes no decent person would wear. Everyone expected Annie to be bad since her father was a wicked thieving gypsy. Bad she was.

But what a sweet tongue she had. Not rough like Tawny's, so smooth and warm. My skin rumpled into goose-prickles along the paths her tongue left wet to the air. But who would complain? This shivering was different from any I'd ever known, quivering in such a strange way that even as my legs prickled I got warmer and warmer. The between-my-legs part felt the most shivery of all. As she moved from my breast to my ribs across my belly I knew that I wanted her to put her mouth there Instead she went down my leg oh under the knees nipping my toes sharp as a cat's then licking my thighs oh my belly my flat nipples oh her tongue sharp on my nipples the between-my-legs part is burning and aching hot but it feels good how can anything that sharp feel good? under my arms and down my arms "Yer s'pose to purr" she says I have been holding my breath obediently I purr between short gasps wanting her to touch between my legs more than ever and wondering at my wish. She turns me over licking and biting along my shoulders and neck purring or growling at me

135

occasionally is this still a game? I cannot bear it and I want her to never stop, her licking at the lower curve of my ass I biting my lip and holding my breath again feeling like I'm about to turn into air or steam. Turning over, "Annie . . ." she shushes me kissing my thighs again she is kissing not licking then she is cautiously pushing my trembling thighs apart looking up into my eyes, "D'ye want to play?" her eyes question see the answer in mine then her tongue touching me I moan she stops, "Did that hurt?" "No" I whisper "please . . ." her tongue touching me again caressing that deep wrinkle of flesh at the center of my cleft. It goes hurt and I feel some deep opening, some emptiness that never felt empty before. Then something happens and I dissolve in wetness tears flowing out of my eyes. I come back to myself clutching her shoulders she lying on top of me propped up on her forearms, looking searchingly into my damp gaze. "Are ye alreet?" I'm not sure what I am but I nod and smile. "Good." Annie huffs down beside me. "Then 'tis my turn to be the kitten and ye be the mumcat."

I soon discovered that I could make Annie melt like she had made me. Her body got very tense as I like her and for a while I thought she was wroth with me 'cause when I reminded her to keep purrin' and she said "Not now!" in a harsh voice. But then she grabbed my hair and pressed my face deeper into her cleft and cried out. I tasted smoke salt flowers and again dissolved.

Later we kissed and solemnly swore to keep our new knowledge a secret. But Annie and I did not know the meaning of the word discretion. Oh, we did not actually talk to anyone about it, and at first probably no one suspected. But as we grew older other villagers began to narrow their eyes at us running down the street holding hands or sauntering in the smithy or at the Inn with our arms around each other.

One day at the smithy watching John Herrick at his trade. Sean, the Laird's son, watching wistfully the smith's skill for he longed to make things with his hands. Several other village men lounging near the forge drinking whisky for comfort against the cold winds. Annie and I with our cloaks around each other, clinging together for warmth, the smokey smell of her hair in my nostrils. The men called for us to sit in their laps share their whisky and get warm. Their laughter is hearty, the lewdness of their interest obvious. I'm no insulted but I'm no tempted neither. Annie feels too good to move. "We're fine as we are," I call back. "Yer too old tae be clinging to each other like snotty-nosed bairns," one joshes. "An' too smart tae be clinging to the likes of you," retorts Annie, kissing me full on the mouth in front of them. We toss our hair like wild horses and canter off through the snow, laughing at the looks on their faces. But while I laugh I feel a cold hard knot in my middle, a fear that someday these men will remember us playing them for fools, and pay us back for it.

John Updike

Couples

F OXY was back in town. The rumor flew from Marcia little-
Smith, who had seen her driving Ken's MG on the Nun's
Bay Road, to Harold to Frank to Janet to Bea and Terry in
the A & P and from there to Carol and the Thornes, to join with the
tributary glimpse Freddy had had of her from his office window as
she emerged that afternoon from Cogswell's Drug Store. The rumor
branched out and began to meet itself in the phrase, "I know";
Terry, acting within, as she guessed at her duties, the office of
confidante that Ken had thrust on the Gallaghers that dawn a
month ago, phoned and gingerly told Angela, who took the news
politely, as if it could hardly concern her. Perhaps it didn't. The
Hanemas had become opaque to other couples, had betrayed the
conspiracy of mutual comprehension. Only Piet, as the delta of
gossip interlaced, remained dry; no one told him. But there was no

need. He already knew. On Tuesday, in care of Gallagher and Hanema, he had received this letter from Washington:

> Dear Piet—
> I must come back to New England for a few days and will be in Tarbox April 24, appropriating furniture. Would you like to meet and talk? Don't be nervous—I have no claims to press.
> Love,
> F.

After "press" the word "but" had been scratched out. They met first by accident, in the town parking lot, an irregular asphalt wilderness of pebbles and parked metal ringed by back entrances to the stores on Charity Street—the A & P, Poirier's Liquor Mart, Beth's Books and Cards, the Methodist Thrift Shop, even via an alleyway sparkling with broken glass, the Tarbox Professional Apartments. He discovered himself unprepared for the sight of her—from a distance, the cadence of her, the dip of her tall body bending to put a shopping bag into her lowslung black car, the blond dab of hair bundled, the sense of the tone of muscle across her abdomen, the vertiginous certainty that it was indeed among the world's billions none other than she. His side hurt; his left palm tingled. He called; she held still in answer, and appeared, closer approached, younger than he had remembered, smoother, and more finely made—the silken skin translucent to her blood, the straight-boned nose faintly paler at the bridge, the brown irises warmed by gold and set tilted in the dainty shelving of her lids, quick lenses subtler than clouds, minutely shutting as she spoke. Her voice dimensional with familiar shadows, the unnumbered curves of her parted, breathing, talking, thinking lips: she was alive. Having lived with frozen fading bits of her, he was not prepared for her to be so alive, so continuous and witty.

"Piet, you look touchingly awful."

"Unlike you."

"Why don't you comb your hair anymore?"

"You even have a little tan."

"My stepfather has a swimming pool. It's summer there."

"It's been off and on here. The same old tease. I've been walking on the beach a lot."

"Why aren't you living with Angela?"

"Who says I'm not?"

"She says. She told me over the phone. Before I wrote you I called your house; I was going to say my farewells to you both."

"She never told me you called."

"She probably didn't think it was very important."

"A mysterious woman, my wife."

"She said I was to come and get you."

He laughed. "If she said that, why did you ask why I wasn't living with her?"

"Why aren't you?"

"She doesn't want me to."

"That's only," Foxy said, "half a reason."

With this observation their talk changed key; they became easier, more trivial, as if a decision had been put behind them. Piet asked her, "Where are you taking the groceries?"

"They're for me. I'm living in the house this weekend. Ken's promised to stay in Cambridge."

"You and Ken aren't going to be reconciled?"

"He's happy. He says he works evenings now and thinks he's on to something significant. He's back on starfish."

"And you?"

She shrugged, a pale-haired schoolgirl looking for the answer broad enough to cover her ignorance. "I'm managing."

"Won't it depress you living there alone? Or do you have the kid?"

"I left Toby with Mother. They get along beautifully, they both think I'm untrustworthy, and adore cottage cheese."

He asked her simply, "What shall we do?" adding in explanation, "A pair of orphans."

He carried her bag of groceries up to his room, and they lived the weekend there. Saturday he helped her go through the empty house by the marsh, tagging the tables and chairs she wanted for herself. No one prevented them. The old town catered to their innocence. Foxy confessed to Piet that, foreseeing sleeping with him, she had brought her diaphragm and gone to Cogswell's Drug Store for a new tube of vaginal jelly. As he felt himself under the balm of love grow boyish and wanton, she aged; his first impression of her smoothness and translucence was replaced by the goose-bumped roughness of her buttocks, the gray unpleasantness of her shaved armpits, the backs of her knees, the thickness of her waist since she had had the baby. Her flat feet gave her walking movements, on the bare floor of Piet's dirty oatmeal-walled room, a slouched awkwardness quite unlike the casually springy step with which Angela, her little toes not touching the floor, moved through the rectangular farmhouse with eggshell trim. Asleep, she snuffled, and restlessly crowded him toward the edge of the bed, and sometimes struggled against nightmares. The first morning she woke him with her hands on his penis, delicately tugging the foreskin, her face pinched and blanched by desire. She cried out that her being here with him was wrong, wrong, and fought his entrance of her; and then afterwards slyly asked if it had made it more exciting for him, her pretending to resist. She asked him abrupt questions, such as, Did he still consider himself a Christian? He said he didn't know, he doubted it. Foxy said of herself that she did, though a Christian living in a state of sin; and defiantly, rather arrogantly and—his impression was—prissily, tossed and stroked back her hair, tangled damp from the pillow. She complained that she was hungry. Did he intend just to keep her here screwing until she starved? Her stomach growled.

They ate in the Musquenomenee Luncheonette, sitting in a booth away from the window, through which they spied on Frank Appleby and little Frankie lugging bags of lime and peat moss from the hardware store into Applebys' old maroon Mercury coupe. They saw but were not seen, as if safe behind a one-way mirror. They discussed Angela and Ken and the abortion, never pausing on one topic long enough to exhaust it, even to explore it; the state of their being together precluded discussion, as if, in the end, everything was either too momentous or too trivial. Piet felt, even when they lay motionless together, that they were skimming, hastening through space, lightly interlocked, yet not essentially mingled. He slept badly beside her. She had difficulty coming with him. Despairing of her own climax, she would give herself to him in slavish postures, as if witnessing in her mouth or between her breasts the tripped unclotting thump of his ejaculation made it her own. She still wore the rings of her marriage and engagement, and gazing down to where her hand was guiding him into her silken face, her cheek concave as her jaws were forced apart, he noticed the icy octagon of her diamond and suffered the realization that if they married he would not be able to buy her a diamond so big.

She did not seem to be selling herself; rather, she was an easy and frank companion. After the uncomfortable episode of tagging the furniture (he was not tempted to touch her in this house they had often violated; her presence as she breezed from room to room felt ghostly, impervious; and already they had lost that prerogative of lovers which claims all places as theirs) she walked with him Saturday along the beach, along the public end, where they would not be likely to meet friends. She pointed to a spot where once she had written him a long letter that he had doubtless forgotten. He said he had not forgotten it, though in part he had. She suddenly told him that his callousness, his promiscuity, had this advantage for her; with him she could be as whorish as she wanted, that unlike most men he really didn't judge. Piet answered that it was his Calvinism. Only God judged. Anyway he found her totally beautiful. Totally: bumps, pimples, flat feet, snuffles and all. She laughed to hear herself so described and the quality of her laugh told him she was vain, that underneath all fending disclaimers she thought of herself as flawless. Piet believed her, believed the claim of her barking laugh, a shout snatched away by the salt wind beside the spring sea, her claim that she was in truth perfect, and he hungered to be again with her long body in the stealthy shabby shelter of his room.

Lazily she fellated him while he combed her lovely hair. Oh and lovely also her coral cunt, coral into burgundy, with its pansy-shaped M, or W, of fur: kissing her here, as she unfolded from gateway into chamber, from chamber into universe, was a blind pleasure tasting of infinity until, he biting her, she clawed his back and came. Could break his neck. Forgotten him entirely. All raw self. Machine that makes salt at the bottom of the sea.

Mouths, it came to Piet, are noble. They move in the brain's court. We send our genitals mating down below like peasants, but when the mouth condescends, mind and body marry. To eat another is sacred. *I love thee, Elizabeth, thy petaled rankness, thy priceless casket of nothing lined with slippery buds.* Thus on the Sunday morning, beneath the hanging clangor of bells.

"Oh Piet," Foxy sighed to him, "I've never felt so taken. No one has ever known me like this."

Short of sleep, haggard from a month of fighting panic, he smiled and tried to rise to her praise with praise of her, and fell asleep instead, his broad face feverish, as if still clamped between her thighs.

Dan Anderson and
Maggie Berman

Sex Tips for Straight Women from a Gay Man

BJ Basics

Acommon male misconception is that the fuller the lips, the better the blow job. We say any old lips will do. It's not the size, it's what you do with them. These BJ basics are guaranteed to blow his mind as well as his horn.

The key to a good blow job exists just as much in your head as in your hands and mouth. He's allowing you to take control over the most sensitive and precious parts of his body. Deep down he knows that you could knock him off in a nanosecond. Remember, his penis is your friend, and you'll want to give it as much attention as you would your very, very best friend. You really have to show respect and concentrate big time on what you're doing. And he'll know if you're really being friends with Mr. Stiffy, or just being a phony.

We cannot overemphasize the proper state of mind. He wants to feel that you are enthusiastically devoting your talents to making his penis happy, and that you're not just doing it because you had too much to drink. BJs under those circumstances are not memorable for him. This activity requires your full attention.

Our friend Jonathan told us about a date he went on with an older gentleman. They were making out passionately when Jonathan moved south and was about to go down on his date. Much to Jonathan's chagrin he found a mass of gray hair, froze up, and was simply unable to continue. "It was like having sex with my father or something," he told us afterward. If you think the same thing might happen to you, and you have a fear of gray hair, too, we recommended that you just turn off the light. The real point of the story is that people have all kinds of preconceived notions about and associations with BJs and that you should probably jettison them in order to fully enjoy your new sex life.

Although many people would have you believe that the key to BJs is sucking, his penis is no lollipop. The central action is to move the lips in an up and down, or back and forth, motion. What makes this act so delicious is that you can vary the pressure of your lips, take the penis out of your mouth, lick the sides and top, and use your tongue and hands in a variety of ways that will deliver a scintillating series of sensations.

The building blocks of BJs consist of mouth only, mouth and tongue, and mouth and hands. Building with these blocks is your quickest route to a Park Avenue penthouse. Don't take the power of a blow job lightly. Know what to do, and when and how to do it. Whether it's the overture, the entr'acte or the grand finale, the BJ rightly deserves a place of honor in your sexual repertoire.

If you're starting with Mr. Softee, you should have no trouble putting the whole thing in your mouth while you gently suck and lick. Don't start moving your mouth up and down until he's at least semierect. As with your hand job technique, making a ring around the base of the shaft will help make him hard quicker. And Mr. Softee will turn into Mr. Stiffy in no time.

Before you really get into it, take a sip from your handy glass of water. Kneel between his legs so you can show respect for his prized possession. Put both hands into the L position around the base of the shaft. Lick the whole tip, and then use your tongue to lick up and down the sides. Now it should be slick enough to slide into your mouth easily. Covering your teeth with your lips, and keeping your mouth taut, glide the head inside and lick the sensitive spot underneath with both the tip and flat part of your tongue. Amateurs may think they should use a snakelike quickie lick, but your lick should be more like what you would use on your favorite flavor of ice cream cone.

Still covering your teeth, and maintaining your pressure, proceed down the shaft as far as you can go in one fell swoop. Women usually think it's better to go up and down, letting a little more into their mouths each time. That's for amateurs. Let him know right away that you're going to take good care of him. Relax the muscles in your neck and jaw as much as possible. Try to breathe through your nose. Being in this position allows you to control how far in it goes. Pull your mouth back up the entire length of the shaft, right over the ridge of the tip. Just as in the ring technique of the hand job, he'll love the sensation of your lips popping over the ridge. Take it out of your mouth for a second, and go straight back down. This will give you a chance to breathe,

Continue the full up-and-down-the-entire-shaft motion at a sensual, slow pace. Once you get bored with this, usually after two to three minutes, it's time to start using your hand. One hand will always remain at the base of the penis to keep it in place. With the other hand, make a ring with your thumb and forefinger, and follow the motion of your lips up and down. Maintain the slow pace. Remember to breathe when you get to the top. When you're ready to make him really moan, switch from the ring to the magic upstroke, twist, over and down technique, combining a hand stroke with a mouth stroke. Coordinating these motions will take some practice, but it will be well worth it. Still keep the pace slow and steady, or it may be over before you know it.

Don't forget to pay attention to his nipples, if he likes that. This will give you something else to concentrate on so you don't get bored, and it will feel great for him. Let your hands work their magic on his penis for a bit, while you use your mouth on his inner thighs, balls, lower stomach and that sensitive spot where his legs meet his body. Try licking this area first to soften it up, then use your lips to lightly squeeze and massage it. Once you get really good at this, you can have your mouth on his shaft while one hand tweaks his nipples and the other holds his balls.

We recommend torturing him a bit to remind him just how good you really are. You can, in fact you should, pause in the middle of a blow job any time you feel like it. Stop what you're doing. Remove your hand and mouth, and move back up his stomach and chest to his face. Planting a couple of kisses on his lips, neck and shoulders about now will let him cool down for a few minutes. Stopping, starting, stopping and starting again will make for a bigger, better and much more powerful orgasm.

After you've stopped and started a few times, and you've got him just about ready to burst, return to the upstroke, twist, over and down—mouth combo, working in some head rub action and go into a fast ring technique—mouth combo. Gay men who at one time had sex with women say the difference is that women rarely go hard and fast enough toward the end. We're not telling you to get sloppy, just build up the crescendo to a rousing climax. When he's ready to let it rip, move your head out of the way, or prepare to swallow—more on this later. Keep stroking with your hand until it's over. Don't forget to let go after the first few spurts. It's a rare guy who likes his penis held immediately after ejaculation. Now might be an excellent time to mention an engagement ring, or suggest that trip to Paris you've been wanting.

Last Word

Perhaps your biggest concern about the world's best BJ is gagging. Well, there are times when smaller can be infinitely more manageable. There is no surefire way we know of to completely prevent gagging every time. A lot of it has to do with your relaxation level, and how comfortable you feel. A lot has to do with the control of your breathing. The tips in this book are designed to make you feel confident and in control no matter what you are doing, or with whom you are doing it. Relax your muscles. Your first reaction when a hot rod is heading toward the back of your throat is to tense up. Remember that Mr. Stiffy is your friend and that he will only feel as comfortable as you do. Also, the less your neck and head are bent, the more room you will have to fit his penis inside your mouth. The best way to prevent gagging is to coordinate your breathing with the in-and-out movements. Take a deep breath in while you can, then release it through your nose as you go back down on your partner.

A Note on Swallowing

Gay men never swallow. Yes, you heard it here, and it may not be true 100 percent of the time, but for the most part, they don't. Besides being somewhat unsafe, it also takes away the thrill of seeing someone ejaculate. We know that to some of you, that thrill is on par with seeing a *National Geographic* special on penguins, and Maggie insists that she gets absolutely nothing out of seeing a man come. Swallowing for women is a thorny issue. Some straight men make a big deal out of it, but that seems inconsequential to us. Without getting into a whole big discussion on the power politics of swallowing, we're here to tell you that you should never do anything you don't want to. If you choose to swallow, that is your decision. If you choose not to, then you certainly have nothing to apologize for. Especially since you will have just given him the most spectacular, mind-blowing, spine-tingling BJ he's ever had.

Afterword

Gay men generally don't worry about this, but some women we know are concerned about "dick breath" when they kiss their

partner after going down on him. This is another of those precon-
ceptions that you should really let go of. Assuming you're both tidy
and have showered within a reasonable amount of time, you shouldn't
have too much to worry about. If you're absolutely nuts about it, try
taking a sip of water or wine before kissing him. And if he thinks
it's gross, just remember that it was his dick, after all.

Harold Brodkey

Innocence

ONE afternoon, things went well for us. We went for a walk, the air was plangent, there was the amazed and polite pleasure we had sometimes merely at being together. Orra adjusted her pace now and then to mine; and I kept mine adjusted to her most of the time. When we looked at each other, there would be small, soft puffs of feeling as of toy explosions or sparrows bathing in the dust. Her willed softness, her inner seriousness or earnestness, her strength, her beauty, muted and careful now in her anxiety not to lose me yet, made the pleasure of being with her noble, contrapuntal, and difficult in that one had to live up to it and understand it and protect it, against my clumsiness and Orra's falsity, kind as that falsity was; or the day would become simply an exploitation of a strong girl who would see through that sooner or later and avenge it. But things went well;

and inside that careless and careful goodness, we went home; we screwed; I came—to get my excitement out of the way; she didn't know I was doing that; she was stupendously polite; taut; and very admiring. "How pretty you are," she said. Her eyes were blurred with half-tears. I'd screwed without any fripperies, coolly, in order to leave in us a large residue of sexual restlessness but with the burr of immediate physical restlessness in me removed: I still wanted her; I always wanted Orra; and the coming had been dull; but my body was not very assertive, was more like a glove for my mind, for my will, for my love for her, for my wanting to make her feel more.

She was slightly tearful, as I said, and gentle, and she held me in her arms after I came, and I said something like "Don't relax. I want to come again," and she partly laughed, partly sighed, and was flattered, and said, "Again? That's nice." We had a terrific closeness, almost like a man and a secretary—I was free and powerful, and she was devoted: there was little chance Orra would ever be a secretary—she'd been offered executive jobs already for when she finished college—but to play at being a secretary who had no life of her own was a romantic thing for Orra. I felt some apprehension, as before a game of tennis that I wanted to win, or as before stealing something off a counter in a store: there was a dragging enervation, a fear and silence, and there was a lifting, a preparation, a willed and then unwilled, self-contained fixity of purpose; it was a settled thing; it would happen.

After about ten minutes or so, perhaps it was twenty, I moved in her: I should say that while I'd rested, I'd stayed in her (and she'd held on to me). As I'd expected—and with satisfaction and pride that everything was working, my endowments were cooperating— I felt my prick come up; it came up at once with comic promptness, but it was sore—Jesus, was it sore. It, its head, ached like hell, with a dry, burning, reddish pain.

The pain made me chary and prevented me from being excited except in an abstract way; my mind was clear; I was idly smiling as I began, moving very slowly, just barely moving, sore of pressing on her inside her, moving around, lollygagging around, feeling out the reaches in there, arranging the space inside her, as if to put the inner soft-oiled shadows in her in order; or like stretching out your hand in the dark and pressing a curve of a blanket into familiarity or to locate yourself when you're half asleep, when your eyes are closed. In fact, I did close my eyes and listened carefully to her breathing, concentrating on her but trying not to let her see I was doing that because it would make her self-conscious.

Her reaction was so minimal that I lost faith in fucking for getting her started, and I thought I'd better go down on her; I pulled out of her, which wasn't too smart, but I wasn't thinking all that consequentially; she'd told me on other occasions she didn't like "all that foreign la-di-da," that it didn't excite her, but I'd always thought it was only that she was ashamed of not coming and that made being gone down on hard for her. I started in on it; she protested; and I pooh-poohed her objections and did it anyway; I was raw with nerves, with stifled amusement because of the lying and the tensions, so much of it. I remarked to her that I was going down on her for my own pleasure; I was jolted by touching her with my tongue there when I was so raw-nerved, but I hid that. It seemed to me physical unhappiness and readiness were apparent in her skin—my lips and tongue carried the currents of a jagged unhappiness and readiness in her into me; echoes of her stiffness and dissatisfaction sounded in my mouth, my head, my feet; my entire tired body was a stethoscope. I was entirely a stethoscope; I listened to her with my *bones;* the glimmers of excitement in her traveled to my *spine;* I felt her grinding sexual haltedness, like a car's broken starter motor grinding away in her, in my *stomach,* in my *knees.* Every part of me listened to her; every goddamned twinge of muscular contraction she had that I noticed or that she should have had because I was licking her clitoris and she didn't have, every testimony of excitement or of no-excitement in her, I listened for so hard it was amazing it didn't drive her out of bed with self-consciousness; but she probably couldn't tell what I was doing, since I was out of her line of sight, was down in the shadows, in the basement of her field of vision, in the basement with her sexual feelings where they lay, strewn about.

When she said, "No . . . No, Wiley . . . Please don't. No . . . " and wiggled, although it wasn't the usual pointless protest that some girls might make—it was real, she wanted me to stop—I didn't listen because I could feel she responded to my tongue more than she had to the fucking a moment before. I could feel beads sliding and whispering and being strung together rustlingly in her; the disorder, the scattered or strewn sexual bits, to a very small extent were being put in order. She shuddered. With discomfort. She produced, was subjected to, her erratic responses. And she made odd, small cries, protests mostly, uttered little exclamations that mysteriously were protests although they were not protests, too, cries that somehow suggested the ground of protest kept changing for her.

I tried to string a number of those cries together, to cause them to occur in a mounting sequence. It was a peculiar attempt: it seemed we moved, I moved with her, on dark water, between two lines of buoys, dark on one side, there was nothingness there, and on the other, lights, red and green, the lights of the body advancing on sexual heat, the signs of it anyway, nipples like scored pebbles, legs lightly thrashing, little ohs; nothing important, a body thing; you go on: you proceed.

When we strayed too far, there was nothingness, or only a distant flicker, only the faintest guidance. Sometimes we were surrounded by the lights of her responses, widely spaced, bobbing unevenly, on some darkness, some ignorance we both had, Orra and I, of what were the responses of her body. To the physical things I did and to the atmosphere of the way I did them, to the authority, the argument I made that this was sexual for her, that the way I touched her and concentrated on her, on that partly dream-laden dark water or underwater thing, she responded; she rested on that, rolled heavily on that. Everything I did was speech, was hiero-glyphics, pictures on her nerves; it was what masculine authority was for, was what bravery and a firm manner and musculature were supposed to indicate that a man could bring to bed. Or skill at dancing; or musicianliness; or a sad knowingness. Licking her, holding her belly, stroking her belly pretty much with unthoughtout movements—sometimes just moving my fingers closer together and spreading them again to show my pleasure, to show how rewarded I felt, not touching her breasts or doing any-thing so intensely that it would make her suspect me of being out to make her come—I did those things but it seemed like I left her alone and was private with my own pleasures. She felt unobserved with her sensations, she had them without responsibility, she clutched at them as something round and slippery in the water, and she would fall off them, occasionally gasping at the loss of her balance, the loss of her self-possession, too.

I'd flick, idly almost, at her little spaghetti-ending with my tongue, then twice more idly, then three or four or five times in sequence, then settle down to rub it or bounce it between lip and tongue in a steadily more earnest way until my head, my consciousness, my lips and tongue were buried in the dark of an ascending and concentrated rhythm, in the way a stoned dancer lets a movement catch him and wrap him around and become all of him, become his voyage and not a collection of repetitions at all.

Then some boring stringy thing, a sinew at the base of my tongue, would begin to ache, and I'd break off that movement, and sleepily lick her, or if the tongue was too uncomfortable, I'd worry her clit, I'd nuzzle it with my pursed lips until the muscles that held my lips pursed grew tired in their turn; and I'd go back and flick at her tiny clitoris with my tongue, and go on as before, until the darkness came; she sensed the darkness, the privacy for her, and she seemed like someone in a hallway, unobserved, moving her arms, letting her mind stroke itself, taking a step in that dark.

But whatever she felt was brief and halting; and when she seemed to halt or to be dead or jagged, I authoritatively, gesturally accepted that as part of what was pleasurable to me and did not let it stand as hint or foretaste of failure; I produced sighs of pleasure, even gasps, not all of them false, warm nuzzlings, and caresses that indicated I was rewarded—I produced rewarded strokings; I made elements of sexual pleasure out of moments that were unsexual and that could be taken as the collapse of sexuality.

And she couldn't contradict me because she thought I was working on my own coming, and she loved me and meant to be cooperative.

What I did took nerve because it gave her a tremendous ultimate power to laugh at me, although what the courtship up until now had been for was to show that she was not an enemy, that she could control the hysteria of fear or jealousy in her or the cold judgments in her of me that would lead her to say or do things that would make me hate or fear her; what was at stake included the risk that I would look foolish in my own eyes—and might then attack her for failing to come—and then she would be unable to resist the inward conviction that I was a fool. Any attempted act confers vulnerability on you, but an act devoted to her pleasure represented doubled vulnerability since only she could judge it; and I was safe only if I was immune or insensitive to her; but if I was immune or insensitive I could not hope to help her come; by making myself vulnerable to her, I was in a way being a sissy or a creep because Orra wasn't organized or trained or prepared to accept responsibility for how I felt about myself: she was a woman who wanted to be left alone; she was paranoid about the inroads on her life men in their egos tried to make: there was dangerous masochism, dangerous hubris, dangerous hopefulness, and a form of love in my doing what I did: I nuzzled nakedly at the crotch of the sexual tigress; any weakness in her ego or her judgment and she would lash out at *me;* and the line was very frail between what I was doing as love and as intrusion, exploitation, and stupid boastfulness. There was no way for me even to begin to imagine the mental pain—or the physical pain—for her if I should fail and, to add to that, if I should withdraw from her emotionally, too, because of my failure and hers and our pain. Or merely because the failure might make me so uncomfortable I couldn't go on unless she nursed my ego, and she couldn't nurse my ego, she didn't know how to do it, and probably was inhibited about doing it.

Sometimes my hands, my fingers, not just the tops, but all of their inside surface and the palms, held her thighs, or cupped her little belly, or my fingers moved around the lips, the labia or what-ever, or even poked a little into her, or with the nails or tips lightly nudged her clitoris, always within a fictional frame of my absolute sexual pleasure, of my admiration for this sex, of there being no danger in it for us. No tongues or brains handy to speak unkindly, I meant. My God, I felt exposed and noble. This was a great effort to make for her.

Perhaps that only indicates the extent of my selfishness. I didn't mind being feminized except for the feeling that Orra would not ever understand what I was doing but would ascribe it to the power of my or our sexuality. I minded being this self-conscious and so conscious of her; I was separated from my own sexuality, from any real sexuality; a poor sexual experience, even one based on love, would diminish the ease of my virility with her at least for a while; and she wouldn't understand. Maybe she would become much subtler and shrewder sexually and know how to handle me, but that wasn't likely. And if I apologized or complained or explained in that problematic future why I was sexually a little slow or reluctant with her, she would then blame my having tried to give her orgasm, she would insist I must not be bored again, so I would in that problematic future, if I wanted her to come, have to lie and say I was having more excitement than I felt, and that, too, might diminish my pleasure. I would be deprived even of the chance for honesty: I would be further feminized in that regard. I thought all this while I went down on her. I didn't put it in words but thought in great misty blocks of something known or sensed. I felt an inner weariness I kept working in spite of. This ignoring myself gave me an odd, starved feeling, a mixture of agony and helplessness. I didn't want to feel like that. I suddenly wondered why in the theory of relativity the speed of light is given as a constant: was that more Jewish absolutism? Surely in a universe as changeable and as odd as this one, the speed of light, considering the variety of experiences, must vary; there must be a place where one could see a beam of light struggle to move. I felt silly and selfish; it couldn't be avoided that I felt like that—I mean, it couldn't be avoided by *me*.

Whatever she did when I licked her, if she moved at all, if a muscle twitched in her thigh, a muscle twitched in mine, my body imitated hers as if to measure what she felt or perhaps for no reason but only because the sympathy was so intense. The same things happened to each of us but in amazingly different contexts, as if we stood at opposite ends of the room and reached out to touch each other and to receive identical messages which then diverged as they entered two such widely separated sensibilities and two such divergent and incomplete ecstasies. The movie we watched was of her discovering how her sexual responses worked: we were seated far apart. My tongue pushed at her erasure, her wronged and heretofore hardly existent sexual powers. I stirred her with varieties of kisses far from her face. A strange river moved slowly, bearing us along, reeds hid the banks, willows braided and unbraided themselves, moaned and whispered, raveled and faintly clicked. Orra groaned, sighed, shuddered, shuddered harshly or liquidly; sometimes she jumped when I changed the pressure or posture of my hands on her or when I rested for a second and then resumed. Her body jumped and contracted interestingly but not at any length or in any pattern that I could understand. My mind grew tired. There is a limit to invention, to mine anyway: I saw myself (stupidly) as a Roman trireme, my tongue as the prow, *bronze*, pushing at her; she was the Mediterranean. Tiers of slaves—my God, the helplessness of them—pulled oars, long stalks that metaphorically and rhythmically bloomed with flowing clusters of short-lived lilies at the water's surface. The pompous and out-of-proportion boat, all of me hunched over Orra's small sea—not actually hunched: what I was was lying flat; the foot of the bed was at my waist or near there, my legs were out, my feet were propped distantly on the floor, all of me was concentrated on the soft, shivery, furry delicacies of Orra's twat—the pompous boat advanced lickingly, leaving a trickling, gurgling wake of half response, the ebbing of my will and activity into that fluster subsiding into the dark water of this girl's passivity, taut storminess, and self ignorance.

The whitish bubbling, the splash of her discontinuous physical response: those waves, ah, that wake rose, curled outward, bubbled, and fell. Rose, curled outward, bubbled, and fell. The white fell of a naiad. In the vast spreading darkness and silence of the sea. There was nothing but that wake. The darkness of my senses when the rhythm absorbed me (so that I vanished from my awareness, so that I was blotted up and was a stain, a squid hidden, stroking Orra) made it twilight or night for me; and my listening for her pleasure, for our track on that markless ocean, gave me the sense that where we were was in a lit-up, great, ill-defined oval of night air and sea and opalescent fog, rainbowed where the lights from the portholes of an immense ship were altered prismatically by droplets of mist—as in some 1930s movie, as in some dream. Often I was out of breath; I saw spots, colors, ocean depths. And her protests, her doubts! My God, her doubts! Her, *No don't, Wiley*s and her *I don't want to do this*es and her *Wiley, don't*s and *Wiley, I can't come— don't do this—I don't like this*es. Mostly I ignored her. Sometimes I silenced her by leaning my cheek on her belly and watching my hand stroke her belly and saying to her in a sex-thickened voice, "Orra, I like this—this is for me."

Then I went down on her again with unexpectedly vivid, real pleasure, as if merely thinking about my own pleasure excited and refreshed me, and there was yet more pleasure, when she—reassured or strengthened by my putative selfishness, by the conviction that this was all for me, that nothing was expected of her—cried out. Then a second later she *grunted*. Her whole body rippled. Jesus, I loved it when she reacted to me. It was like causing an entire continent to convulse, Asia, South America. I felt huge and tireless.

In her excitement, she threw herself into the air, but my hands happened to be on her belly; and I fastened her down, I held that part of her comparatively still, with her twat fastened to my mouth, and I licked her while she was in midheave; and she yelled; I kept my mouth there as if I were drinking from her; I stayed like that until her upper body fell back on the bed and bounced, she made the whole bed bounce; then my head bounced away from her; but I still held her down with my hands; and I fastened myself, my mouth, on her twat again; and she yelled in a deep voice, *"Wiley, what are you doing!"*

Her voice was deep, as if her impulses at that moment were masculine, not out of neurosis but in generosity, in an attempt to improve on the sickliness she accused women of; she wanted to meet me halfway, to share; to share my masculinity: she thought men were beautiful. She cried out, *"I don't want you to do things to me! I want you to have a good fuck!"*

Her voice was deep and despairing, maybe with the despair that goes with surges of sexuality, but then maybe she thought I would make her pay for this. I said, "Orra, I like this stuff, this stuff is what gets me excited." She resisted, just barely, for some infinitesimal fragment of a second, and then her body began to vibrate; it twittered as if in it were the strings of a musical instrument set jangling; she said foolishly —but sweetly—"Wiley, I'm embarrassed, Wiley, this embarrasses me . . . Please stop. . . . No . . . No . . . No . . . Oh . . . Oh . . . Oh . . . I'm very sexual, I'm too sexual to have orgasms, Wiley, stop, please. . . . Oh . . . Oh . . . Oh . . ." And then a deeper shudder ran through her; she gasped; then there was a silence; then she gasped again; she cried out in an extraordinary voice, "I FEEL SOMETHING!" The hair stood up on the back of my neck; I couldn't stop; I hurried on; I heard a dim moaning come from her. What had she felt before? I licked hurriedly. How unpleasant for her, how unreal and twitchy had the feelings been that I'd given her? In what way was this different? I wondered if there was in her a sudden swarming along her nerves, a warm conviction of the reality of sexual pleasure. She heaved like a whale—no: not so much as that. But it was as if half an ocean rolled off her young flanks; some element of darkness vanished from the room; some slight color of physical happiness tinctured her body and its thin coating of sweat; I felt it all through me; she rolled on the surface of a pale blue, a pink and blue sea; she was dark and gleaming, and immense and wet. And warm.

She cried, *"Wiley, I feel a lot!"*

God, she was happy.

I said, "Why not?" I wanted to lower the drama quotient; I thought the excess of drama was a mistake, would overburden her. But also I wanted her to defer to me, I wanted authority over her body now, I wanted to make her come.

But she didn't get any more excited than that: she was rigid, almost boardlike after a few seconds. I licked at her thing as best I could but the sea was dry; the board collapsed. I faked it that I was very excited; actually I was so caught up in being sure of myself, I didn't know what I really felt. I thought, as if I were much younger than I was, Boy, if this doesn't work, is my name mud. Then to build up the risk, out of sheer hellish braggadocio, instead of just acting out that I was confident—and in sex, everything unsaid that is portrayed in gestures instead is twice as powerful—when she said, because the feeling was less for her now, the feeling she liked having gone away, "Wiley, I can't—this is silly—" I said, "Shut up, Orra, I know what I'm doing. . . ." But I didn't know.

And I didn't like that tone for sexual interplay either, except as a joke, or as role playing, because pure authority involves pure submission, and people don't survive pure submission except by being slavishly, possessively, vindictively in love; when they are in love like that, they can *give* you nothing but rebellion and submission, bitchiness and submission; it's a general rottenness: you get no part of them out of bed that has any value; and in bed, you get a grudging submission, because what the slave requires is your total attention, or she starts paying you back; I suppose the model is childhood, that slavery. Anyway, I don't like it. But I played at it then, with Orra, as a gamble.

Everything was a gamble. I didn't know what I was doing; I figured it out as I went along; and how much time did I have for figuring things out just then? I felt strained as at poker or roulette, sweaty and a little stupid, placing bets—with my tongue—and waiting to see what the wheel did, risking my money when no one forced me to, hoping things would go my way, and I wouldn't turn out to have been stupid when this was over.

Also, there were sudden fugitive convulsions of lust now, in sympathy with her larger but scattered responses, a sort of immediate and automatic sexuality—I was at the disposal, inwardly, of the sexuality in her and could not help myself, could not hold it back and avoid the disappointments, and physical impatience, the impatience in my skin and prick, of the huge desire that unmistakably accompanies love, of a primitive longing for what seemed her happiness, for closeness to her as to something I had studied and was studying and had found more and more of value in—what was of value was the way she valued me, a deep and no doubt limited (but in the sexual moment it seemed illimitable) permissiveness toward me, a risk she took, an allowance she made as if she'd let me damage her and use her badly.

Partly what kept me going was stubbornness because I'd made up my mind before we started that I wouldn't give up; and partly what it was was the feeling she aroused in me, a feeling that was, to be honest, made up of tenderness and concern and a kind of mere affection, a brotherliness, as if she were my brother, not different from me at all.

Actually this was brought on by an increasing failure, as the sex went on, of one kind of sophistication—of worldly sophistication—and by the increase in me of another kind, of a childish sophistication, a growth of innocence: Orra said, or exclaimed, in a half-harried, half-amazed voice, in a hugely admiring, gratuitous way, as she clutched at me in approval, "Wiley, I never had feelings like these before!"

And to be the first to have caused them, you know? It's like being a collector, finding something of great value, where it had been unsuspected and disguised, or like earning any honor; this partial success, this encouragement gave rise to this pride, this inward innocence.

Of course that lessened the risk for this occasion; I could fail now and still say, *It was worth it,* and she would agree; but it lengthened the slightly longer-term risk; because I might feel trebly a fool someday. Also, it meant we might spend months making love in this fashion—I'd get impotent, maybe not in terms of erection, but I wouldn't look forward to sex—still, that was beautiful to me in a way, too, and exciting. I really didn't know what I was thinking: whatever I thought was part of the sex.

I went on; I wanted to hit the jackpot now. Then Orra shouted, "It's *there*! It's THERE!" I halted, thinking she meant it was in some specific locale, in some specific motion I'd just made with my tired

tongue and jaw; I lifted my head—but couldn't speak: in a way, the
sexuality pressed on me too hard for me to speak; anyway, I didn't
have to; she had lifted her head with a kind of overt twinship and
she was looking at me down the length of her body; her face was
askew and boyish—every feature was wrinkled; she looked angry
and yet naive and swindleable; she said angrily, naively, *"Wiley, it's
there!"*

But even before she spoke that time, I knew she'd meant it was
in her; the fox had been startled from its covert again; she had seen
it, had felt it run in her again. She had been persuaded that it was in
her for good.

Author Biographies

DAN ANDERSON AND MAGGIE BERMAN have been best friends for nine years. They live in New York and Philadelphia.

HAROLD BRODKEY contributed short stories to *The New Yorker, American Review,* and *Esquire* and published two collections: *First Love and Other Sorrows* and *Stories in an Almost Classical Mode,* from which the excerpt appearing here was taken.

LAURA CHESTER has widely published short stories and poetry and has edited several anthologies of women's writing on sexual themes.

KEN CHOWDER has published short stories and the novels *Blackbird Days, Delicate Geometry,* and *Jadis.*

CERRIDWEN FALLINGSTAR has published more than a hundred articles, poems and stories in various newspapers, magazines, and books. *The Heart of the Fire* is her first novel.

FRANK HARRIS was born in Galway in 1854, later becoming a U.S. citizen. He published novels, short stories, and biographies; his autobiography, *My Life and Loves,* was banned in England and the United States for years.

ERICA JONG, a poet and novelist, published *Fear of Flying* in 1973. *Ms.* magazine called her the "first woman to write in such a daring and humorous way about sex."

NORMAN MAILER wrote *The Naked and the Dead* and many other books of fiction and nonfiction. He was also a co-founder of *The Village Voice.*

ANAÏS NIN is best known for her lifelong *Diary*, which she began in 1914. "The Woman on the Dunes" appears in *Little Birds,* which was one of two books of erotica she wrote for a dollar a page in the early 1940s.

ANKA RADAKOVICH lives in New York City and has written a sex column for *Details* magazine since 1990.

JEREMY REED has published almost forty books of poetry, fiction, and nonfiction. He lives in London.

JILL ROBINSON is a novelist and essayist, and the daughter of former MGM executive Dore Schary. Her novels include *Perdido, Bed Time Story,* and *Star Country.*

PHILIP ROTH was born in Newark, New Jersey, in 1933. *Portnoy's Complaint* was his third novel; *American Pastoral* and *I Married a Communist* are his most recent.

CHARLES SIMMONS was an editor of the *New York Times Book Review* for more than twenty years. He is the author of five novels, including *Wrinkles, The Belles-Lettres Papers*, and the recently published *Salt Water*.

SUSAN ST. AUBIN's writing has appeared in the magazines *Libido* and *Yellow Silk*, and in several anthologies, including *Yellow Silk: Erotic Arts and Letters, Fever*, and *Best American Erotica 1995*.

GAY TALESE is a widely published journalist and the author of several books, including *Honor Thy Father* and *The Kingdom and the Power*.

JOHN UPDIKE is a prolific novelist, critic, poet, short story writer, essayist, children's book author, playwright, and translator. His most recent book is *Bech at Bay*.

OSCAR WILDE was born in Ireland in 1854. He was a controversial and prolific author of fiction, poetry, plays, and criticism. *Teleny*, an anonymous novel first published in 1893, has been primarily attributed to him.

FRANK ZAPPA was a songwriter, composer, musician, filmmaker, record and film producer, and iconoclast. Peter Occhiogrosso was his collaborator on *The Real Frank Zappa Book*.